GW00865362

1 MONTH OF
FREE
READING

at

www.ForgottenBooks.com

ISBN 978-0-428-96788-8
PIBN 10209848

THE GOLDEN SEASON

BY

MYRA KELLY

Author of "Rosnah," "The Isle of Dreams,"
"Little Citizens," "Wards of Liberty," etc., etc.

Illustrated by R. M. Crosby, H. Heyer and W. Morgan

NEW YORK
DOUBLEDAY, PAGE & COMPANY
1909

The illustrations for "Made in Heaven", and "Usurpation of Office" appeared originally in Appleton's Magazine, and are used through the courtesy of Messrs. D. Appleton & Company. The illustrations for "Elizabeth's Aunt Elizabeth" appeared originally in The American Magazine, and are used by permission of The Phillips Publishing Company.

TO MY ALMA MATER

CONTENTS

ILLUSTRATIONS

THE GOLDEN SEASON

I AM writing this story of Elizabeth Alvord, not because I whole-heartedly approve of her, and certainly not as a guide to the young. My reason is rather that it is my nature to write, and Elizabeth, as I review my acquaintances, seems most worth writing about. Several qualities combined to make her interesting and to set her apart as one of those from whom unusual things might be expected.

She is an orphan, moderately well off. Both her parents were people of importance, almost of fame in the case of her father, an explorer who left his name and his bones on a mile-long island in the Arctic Ocean. Her mother had written poetry still remembered by the critics and still ignored by the public.

"And what?" Elizabeth would demand when my mother mildly chided her for some unusually flagrant outbreak, "what can you expect from such a combination?"

Another reason for my taking Elizabeth for a subject is that I know her so well. All our childhood lives were spent in two white pillared, porticoed houses on the main street of our old-fashioned little town. Our not too extensive grounds adjoined, and the bewildered uncle who had charge of the little orphaned Elizabeth was glad enough to accept help and guidance on his unaccustomed way from my gentle widowed mother. So together we two children endured all the sorrows and shared all the joys of happy American childhood, taking measles or the High School with the same undaunted front; and arriving at the time this story opens at the age of twenty and the position of bachelor girls in New York, watched over by my old nurse, Margaret, and attending a college which would eventually make us teachers and useful members of society.

And again, Elizabeth's personality and appearance make the recording of her adventures an easy and a pleasant task. Since one must keep the heroine in one's mind's eye for constant contemplation, it is well to choose a heroine as good looking, well bred, well dressed, and diverting as Elizabeth Alvord always is. She is tall, yet not overwhelming to one of fewer inches. Her hair is dark, her eyes are dark, and she affects, in dress, dull pinks and blues and greens softened by old lace. She learned the trick from two gowns her uncle brought her from Paris, and she is so clever and her dressmaker so obedient that she always looks quite different from everybody else and yet, in some contradictory way, quite in the fashion.

So you see her — tall and slim and young, with a gentle voice, a provocative eye and a talent for mischief which keeps everyone about her in a turmoil, and with whose manifestations the following pages will largely deal.

The college idea was mine: or rather it was my mother's. She held the very sensible view that every girl should have a profession. As I showed nothing but a shuddering distaste for medicine, and a marked inaptitude for anything else, she arrived by the process of elimination at the decision that I should learn to be a teacher. So I was sent to one of the best training colleges in the country and Margaret was sent with me because my mother objected to the dormitory system — could never be persuaded that the girls were not starved and frozen and allowed to go out in the rain without rubbers and otherwise neglected and ill treated. She arranged, therefore, that I was to have a little flat near the campus and that Margaret should oversee my meals, the steam heat, and my rubbers.

Elizabeth coming scoffingly to visit this *ménage* in the third or fourth month of my occupancy thereof, promptly fell in love with the flat, the life, the work, and the people, and gave her three guardian uncles the first real relief they had known since, as a baby of less than a year old, she had been consigned to their care, by enrolling herself as a student of the college and a member of my tiny household.

For a month or more she was so occupied in "making up" the early work of the year that she had no time for mischief. She says she devoted her talents to superintending Professor Wentworth's amazing courtship of me, but I protest that she had nothing to do with it. That story has nothing to do with hers, and John and I would have discovered that we loved one another without any intervention from anyone.

I was generally, in some sort, party to her escapades. Everyone held me responsible for her, and so, even had she not been so commendably frank, I should have known from the reports of outsiders of her little relaxations from discipline. Only one thing remains to be said: Elizabeth is not in the least ashamed of herself and chortled and chuckled over these "proofs" of her iniquities as though she were still turning a college topsy turvy and proving that it is not only among the angels that there is joy over one sinner that repenteth — though our sinner was not too repentant — more than over ninety and nine just persons which need not repentance.

Finally, if it should occur to the reader that I was not always a mere aloof impersonal chronicler, I can only plead that I never pretended to be so and that if I had been, Elizabeth would never have played Johnson to my Boswell.

II

THE MOTHERS OF EDWARD

Y OU play, do you not?" asked the assistant kindergartner, fluttering up to Elizabeth as she sat reading in the library.

"A waltz or so," Elizabeth admitted, "and I can read simple music."

"Then I wonder," the other went on in an agitated whisper with an eye on the fuming librarian, "if you would be so kind as to act as my substitute this afternoon. I always assist Miss Peters at her mothers' class, but to-day there is to be a lecture which I simply cannot miss. I know Miss Peters will not object if you explain the situation to her. Will you be so very kind?"

"I should be delighted," Elizabeth answered, rising and following the fluttered kindergartner into the hall. And really

she was greatly interested and excited, for
a notice on the bulletin board had daily
puzzled and interested us. "Mothers'
Meetings," it read; "Mother-Play-Study-
Problems. The Ethnical and Ethical Significance of the Folk-Game. Friday afternoons
in the Kindergarten Room. Parents Welcome." The last clause seemed exclusive
of inquisitive young students from the Art
Department, and Elizabeth and I had decided
that we could never hope to play a part —
even the piano score — in the solving of
these Mother-Play-Study-Problems.

"And you will be careful to show no surprise at anything you may observe there,"
the assistant charged her understudy. "You
will, I shall have to request, remove your
cap and gown. If you are called upon to
take part in the games you must not hesitate."

"Of course not. I should like it."

"It will be a great privilege for you to
work, even for one afternoon, with Miss
Peters. You know her?"

"I 've never seen her. But when I explain that you sent me ——"

"She will make you welcome. Miss Peters is a most remarkable woman — a great personality."

Miss Peters was indeed an earnest worker in that school of philosophy which teaches: " 'Tis a wise mother who knows her own child. No mother knows her own child. It is the function of the kindergarten to introduce The Child to the Mother. Therefore every kindergarten teacher should hold a Mothers' Meeting every Friday afternoon or evening."

Miss Peters was an expert in the training of parents. Her talks on "The Duty of the Mother Life" and "The Wife's Place in the Husband's World" had edified many a spinster between San Francisco and Cape Cod, and had diverted many a matron between the St. Lawrence and the Gulf of Mexico.

When she found herself in charge of the experimental kindergarten connected with our college, she sent to the parents of the

seventy-eight babies who formed her morning class urgent invitations to dabble in the
spring, Pierian and Fröbelian, over which
she had the honour to preside. Each invitation concluded with the loophole; "If you
find it impossible to attend in person kindly
hand this card to some friend who will repre-
sent you. It is our aim to get into touch
with the home-life of every child entrusted
to our care."

It is a lamentable fact that every mother
profited by this loophole; that the twenty-
five ladies who formed Miss Peters's class
in Mother-Play-Study-Problems were, to a
man, representative friends. Maiden aunts
were plentiful. Childless neighbours had not
scorned advice. Idle and elderly spinsters
craved it. But the mothers, ignorant and
self-satisfied, remained aloof.

When Elizabeth, having stowed away her
academic garb, reached the kindergarten
room the mother class was already established on its little chairs around the wide,

black circle painted upon the floor. And around the centre of every "mother," where once a waist had been, was a girdle of gay and knotted cord, from whose diverse ends there dangled a notebook, a song book and a long pencil.

Every eye in the room studied Elizabeth's trim frock, and her bewilderment, for no bulletin board and no imagination had prepared her for the scene. Before she had recovered her gravity and offered her explanation, Miss Peters, that expert in parents was greeting her with:

"Why, Mrs. Dowling, this is a pleasure!" And then, in answer to Elizabeth's evident surprise; "You need not wonder that I knew you at once. Edward is so remarkably like you. The eyes are almost identical."

Elizabeth remembering the commands of the assistant kindergartner, thought this to be a variety of folk-game and did her best to play it. "You are very kind," she answered, and then with a quick memory

of Little Lord Fauntleroy and of "Dearest,"
she added, "but I have been proud to think
him like his father also," and thereby verified
the guess of the expert and sentenced the
piano to silence for the afternoon. Miss
Peters was triumphant as she turned to the
mother players.

"Ladies," said she, "this is the mother,
actually the mother, of our dear little Edward.
And her joining us just at this point is most
timely, as it gives me an opportunity of
showing you how a little stranger should be
welcomed by the children already in the
class.   We will ask Mrs. Dowling to assume
the rôle of the little stranger.   Consult your
notebooks on the topic: First morning" —
here was a fluttering of pages as each mother
sought the place — "and pray remember
the importance of making the child's first
hours in the kindergarten atmosphere as
comfortable, natural, and homelike as possible. I cannot insist too strongly upon
this."

While the mothers, donning spectacles and dampening thumbs, looked for the proper form of greeting, Miss Peters turned to Edward's uncomfortable parent and purred:

"What is your name, little girl? We call one another by our Christian names," she added, "What is yours?"

"Elizabeth."

"Elizabeth!" gushed the Expert. "What a pretty ·name! Always, ladies, we must admire the name of the new child!" Then she slid back to her gushing to ask:

"And what shall we say to little Elizabeth? How shall we welcome our little friend?"

The class having put away its spectacles and dried its thumbs, was ready for thè work in hand. Some advocated the singing of "Welcome, Little Traveller; welcome, welcome home"; others voted for the recitation — with gestures — of "Where did you come from, baby dear?" After some discussion they compromised and agreed to do both. So they sang: they recited — with gestures —

while the Little Traveller wondered when she would begin to feel "comfortable, natural and homelike," and to think regretfully — or so she assures me — of me and all I was missing. But not until the mothers had sung themselves into silence and gesticulated themselves into breathlessness was she girded with stationery and established upon the circle.

When the excitement consequent upon the introduction of this real mother had subsided the Expert prepared her class for a further wrestle with the Mother-Play-Study-Problems.

"We are to take up the beautiful old game of Blind Man's Buff this afternoon," she began. "I hope you have all read the reference I gave you on its history and development. Before we begin our actual play I must ask you once more to yield more thoroughly to the kindergarten atmosphere and to throw yourselves into the games with greater abandon. At our last meeting I observed too much maturity in your attitude. I remember that Mrs. Jones showed quite an adult resentment when Miss Smith accidentally threw her into the fireplace. I should have regretted the circumstance had it not served to show the wisdom of that rule of kindergarten practice: Have a fireplace, but never light the fire."

The scarlet Miss Smith smoothed the agitated bonnet-strings upon her capacious bosom. Mrs. Jones, across the circle, drew herself so suddenly erect that an over-tired kindergarten chair went to its long home. When she had been lifted by the hastily summoned janitor, soothed by Miss Peters, dusted by her neighbours and deposited upon an adult chair by her own determination, the Expert resumed:

"You remember that in our first talk I gave you a list of the firms from which kindergarten equipment might be obtained." There was more fluttering of notebooks and adjusting of glasses. "From that list we shall now strike off the name of Wood, Buckle & Company, who furnished this room."

All the mothers looked uneasy and seemed to derive but fugitive comfort from the proximity of the floor. Miss Peters turned to propitiate further the still indignant Mrs. Jones, and the playful mothers were left to their own devices.

"You may use my notes until you have some of your own," wheezed the little friend upon Elizabeth's right. "I'm Miss Tompkins, but she, Professor Peters, calls me Tommy, because she must have a male element in the games. My nephew, Charlie, is in her morning class. I am sorry that he bit your little Edward's ear last week, but that is Charlie's nature. He has a dominant personality, and Edward should have given the mechanical dog to his little friend."

"Of course," Edward's complacent parent acquiesced. "I shall see that he does so."

"It might be best. Charlie is so modern.

He is always reaching out for new ideas, new sensations ——"

"I fear," began the gentle-faced olive branch in mild spectacles and a jetted cape who towered on Elizabeth's left —"I fear that he got a new sensation when my niece, Gwendoline, stuck a pair of scissors into his leg."

"Your niece!" echoed Miss Tompkins, repenting of earlier kindness: "I had no idea that that insufferable child was a niece of yours. And I want to tell you ladies right here and now that the other children in this kindergarten must give way to my nephew. The dominant note in Charlie cannot be silenced."

But Miss Tompkins was — by a glare from Miss Peters who had now somewhat assuaged the injured Mrs. Jones and persuaded her to wait until the conclusion of the exercises and the serving of refreshments before sending for a policeman. The glare was followed according to the principle of force with gentleness, by the caressing question:

"Would n't Tommy like to tell all the little ones the pretty story he is telling to Elizabeth?"

The children bent lack-lustre eyes upon Tommy, who turned the. pages of his song book with a fat and trembling hand, and the tense silence served as an admirable background for another childish confidence which rent the air.

"I doctored and I doctored," babbled a rosy cherub in a golf-cape and a bonnet, "until my bills were enormous. But no one seemed to know where the real trouble was. I lost every scrap of appetite and I gained a pound a week."

"Did you try electric vibratory massage and mud baths?" asked her neighbour. "They helped me when ——"

But Miss Peters was quick to quell this breach of discipline.

"You will please obey my next words instantly," she commanded. "Are we all ready? One, two, three, *stand!*"

Well, three of the mothers did. So did Miss Peters, who though plump, had retained from slimmer days the art of rising from a very low chair. And yet the mothers did their best. Some were nearly perpendicular before they went crashing back; some knew the impossible when they saw it and extended pleading hands to their more upright comrades. Miss Peters and the three mothers earliest erect — Mrs. Dowling, "Edward's mother," was one of them — did valiant rescue work, shedding hairpins and dislocating belts as they emulated the derrick and wished for the janitor. When the little ones were at last vertical the floor was seen to be strewn with further evidence of the untrustworthiness of Messrs. Wood and Buckle, together with a box of cough drops, four handkerchiefs, two chatelaine bags, an umbrella and three pairs of spectacles.

"We shall not take our work in the prescribed order," announced Miss Peters when the debris had been reclaimed or removed, and the mothers, fanning lustily with note-books, were ready for more instruction. "After the morning circle the 'busy work' rightly comes, but we must sit at our little tables for that, and it seems best to play our games now that we are standing. And let me repeat that I want you all to unbend; to throw yourselves more thoroughly into the play spirit; to yield to the influence of the environment; to relax. When you are told to sit upon the floor I want your obedience to be prompt and happy." The mothers began to look uneasy. "The same rule applies to your rising." Three mothers retreated from the circle, and Edward's parent, struggling with her loosened hair, did not regret them. "When you sing it must be lightly, brightly, and clearly." Two mothers with asthma and one with a gurgling bronchitis faded away. "You are to show in all things the sweet abandonment of childhood and its tense absorption in its play."

A grim determination to be playful lowered upon every brow as the class gathered closely about the wide circle and sang:

" We now for play are ready,
    Our little hands and faces neat;
And so upon the circle,
    We put our little feet."

"Very well indeed," Miss Peters approved. "Does Elizabeth know that pretty song? Would she like her little friends to sing it again?"

"Oh, please, yes," Elizabeth pleaded. "It is beautiful, wonderful; I never heard anything like it."

The mothers — obediently abandoned — repeated their efforts, and the patent leathers of Edward's parent clicked in unison with more commodious shoes as the mothers chanted, panted, and planted their little feet upon the circle.

"Would you mind" — puffed Tommy — "would you mind telling me where my feet are?"

"I beg your pardon," said the amazed newcomer. "You asked ——"

"Where are my feet? Are they on the line? Please see. I can't," and she exhibited a wealth of white stocking, trickling over the footgear technically known as "sister's shoes." "Which way shall I move them? Where is that line?"

"Back a little," Mrs. Dowling advised unsteadily. "Not so much. Now they're right. Keep quiet."

"If she'd only let us!" sighed Gwendoline's aunt. "But the 'tripping lightly to and fro' is the hardest part of these games. You get your feet off and you don't know it, and you can't get them on again."

Still more unsteadily Elizabeth sympathized with such a state while the mothers shuffled and joined hands preparatory to the skipping stage of their development. When they had tripped so lightly and so long as to be incapable of speech or comment, Miss Peters grew didactic again:

"You remember my talk upon The Child's craving for physical expression and the games most suited to that expression. We will take up some of these games this afternoon." With the dexterity of a ventriloquist she slid into her morning manner and purred: "Are all our little feet on the circle? You know Miss Peters cannot play pretty games with careless boys and girls who take their feet off."

"Where are mine?" begged Miss Tompkins in an agony of marking time; "she seems to be looking at mine."

"And I know," Miss Peters cooed, "that you all want to play games. I can tell it by your merry faces."

Then, with wonderful sharpness, she rapped out, "John, Mrs. Johnstone, your feet please!" and the nursery pet whose weight and whose doctor's fees had mounted hand in hand sprang into the aimless agitation of a jumping-jack whose heart-strings are being plucked out by the roots. Finding that

John was quite unable to orientate his invisible feet, Miss Peters craftily suggested:

"Shall we ask our little Johnny to step into the centre and choose the game he would like to play with us?"

Johnny, in helpless embarrassment, ambled into the smaller circle painted in the centre of the larger one and consulted his notebook with one indignant and one tearful eye, while his playfellows sang, in glad chorus:

"Look at our Johnny who chooses our game,
Look at our Johnny, and we'll do the same."

Which they certainly did. "Much too stout for a habit-back skirt," one artless little friend prattled to another.

"And those ruffles over the shoulders are becoming only to slender figures," commented the woman on the other side of her, while John's rising embarrassment grew to wrath and she announced her choice.

"Birdies in the Greenwood," was to be the game. "And I want Mrs. Bancroft" — and she glared at her first critic in all the

warm splendour of a scarlet bodice — "I
want Mrs. Bancroft to be the papa bird
because he was always so brightly coloured
and so beautiful," and Edward's parent made
a rapid entry in her notebook, "first blood
for John, betting even."

The papa bird, so bright and beautiful,
stood solemnly in the inner circle, which was
now "visualized" as a bird's nest, and all
his little comrades, hand lovingly in hand,
skipped past him and warbled, lightly, brightly
and clearly, the tale of his courtship and love.
It was his pleasing privilege, they told him,
to select his mate, the mamma bird. Thrice
did he seal a revolving mother with his favour
and thrice was he repulsed, so that Miss
Peters was obliged to repeat her plea for a
greater yielding to the environment: still more
abandonment in the childishness of these
childless ones. Finally Miss Tompkins was
persuaded to assume the maternal responsibility — in imagination and a bird's nest —
and again the circle hopped and sang, urging

the mamma bird to select three of her friends to be the little blue eggs in the nest.

But this honour was even more violently disclaimed than the other had been. And no one beholding the avoirdupois of the mother bird, could have escaped the impression that the eggs brooded over by her were in danger of becoming an omelette. It was therefore with something very like alarm that Elizabeth saw the electing finger, or claw, pointing in her direction.

"Oh, thank you very much!" she cried. "But really ——"

"We are children," Miss Peters warned her. And she, yielding to the influence of the environment, yielding, too, to the temptation of the moment, struck knuckle into eye and wailed. "Don't want to be an egg. Won't be no nassy egg. Don't want to be squa-aa-ashed. Go 'way!"

She expected instant ejection. Elizabeth Alvord's imitation of a child in the last stages of temper, lisp, stutter and cold in the head

had never been well received by those in
authority over her. But Miss Peters greeted
it appreciatively, and, in the blankness of
her suprise, Mrs. Dowling was led unpro-
testing to the nest. There she, in company
with two other blue eggs, crouched upon the
floor, while the papa and mamma birds
waved their arms — they now called them
wings — and, assisted lightly, brightly and
clearly by the whole skipping class, con-
jured her to hatch into a soft little birdie.
And Edward's parent occupied the period
of her incubation in the amazing calculation
that the nest in the greenwood tree held more
than half a ton of happy bird life.

Presently the circle broke into the glad
tidings that the hatching was accomplished.
The little blue eggs arose — not without
assistance — and proceeded to take flight,
waving arms, dislocating waist-lines and shedding "notions." And as they went the
pictures trembled upon the walls.

"Mrs. Dowling" was enjoying herself. She

had never quite so thoroughly enjoyed herself before. She had stopped for a moment to admire Mrs. Spencer's masterly impersonation of a fledgling, when the birdies, having flown till they were blown, were further interrogated by that insatiable ring:

"What can the little birdies do?"

And the little birdies having reached the articulate stage of their development which ornithologists neglect to mention, panted out:

"We can sing 'Praise the Lord! Sweet May,'" which, as the month was December, and no one's name was even Mary, seemed a bit inconsequent.

"One birdie did not sing her answer," lisped the Expert. "Can the tiniest little baby bird say something to us?" And the tiniest baby bird ran suddenly amuck. Any member of the faculty of that college, especially the men who had charge of the Art Department and its allied branches, could have warned the Expert of the danger of inviting Elizabeth Alvord to cast decorum to the winds and to become as a little child. Whole classes had been dismissed in disorder, because her mood had chanced to be unclassical. No one could restrain her: no lecturer could hold the attention of the other students when she chose to dispute it with him. And here was Miss Peters, actually urging her to be unrestrained in all the consecrated earnestness of a mothers' meeting. The tiniest baby bird swept the circle with a laughing eye and stretched an inviting hand toward Mrs. Jones, seated in still injured majesty apart, and lisped in her imitation of the afflicted infant:

"Baby wants a wumm. Baby wants a wiggly wumm. Jonesy be a wiggly wumm for baby."

Even a maiden aunt, who wrestles with Mother-Play-Study-Problems, may have a dormant sense of humour, and the baffling rage, surprise, and dignity with which Mrs. Jones regarded the seeming innocent figure of Edward's parent, were too much for the gravity of Miss Tompkins. She smiled. Four of the mothers undulated with placid amusement. Laughter threatened the whole circle, and Miss Peters grasped control of the situation just as it was slipping from her. She announced that Genevieve would choose a new game, and Genevieve, having had quite enough exercise for one afternoon, voted for a guessing contest, in which one child shut her eyes very tightly and described some scene lately beheld, while the others guessed its name.

"I see," Genevieve began, in hushed and flute-like tones, "a big, square place, all full of little girls and boys with their mammas and their papas. And I see a good man standing in a high place, and talking to them. And they are all very good, and very happy ——"

"A church!" cried the highly imaginative parents.

Mother after mother closed her eyes and audibly communed, while the others listened and guessed, and were restored to breathing power again. And then came Mrs. Dowling's turn:

"I see a big, round place, and there is music, and there are people. And all the elephants are sitting in a circle, and chains are fastened to them."

"Well, really," snorted Mrs. Jones in the background, "really, I must say!"

Elizabeth opened her guileless eyes and regarded the mothers sitting all in a circle, and all with notebooks chained to their sides. "I'm describing the circus," she explained. "Is there anything wrong?"

But the misgiving that they were not quite qualified for the maternal rôle had been growing in the minds of the representative friends ever since the advent of this real mother, and was not easily to be silenced. And though Miss Peters again changed the game — though she exerted all her persuasive power — though she even read aloud a chapter of exhortative philosophy — the spirit of free play did not return. There was a perfunctory attempt at "Who's got the button?" but no one seemed to care who had it, though several ladies discovered that — what with skipping, tripping and flying —they most certainly had not.

And then Mrs. Jones arose. Her new, little friend, Elizabeth, had danced backward upon a most sensitive toe, and had remarked, in answer to expostulation and in conjunction with apology, that worms were not entitled to toes or even to feet. So Mrs. Jones approached the Expert in Parents and remarked, in hurt and audible accents:

"I shall return to your class when you send me word that you have ejected that person," and she pointed a black-cashmered finger at the intruder.

"I would rather let my niece play her folk-games incorrectly than be subjected to the impertinence which I have this day endured."

The next morning Elizabeth Alvord, a little late as was her custom, found a large woman and a small boy standing on the steps of the college building. The woman accosted Elizabeth:

"Do you know a Miss Matilda Peters?" she demanded. "I want to see her." Then to the boy, "Edward, stop crying."

"I have met her," Elizabeth answered with a horrible misgiving growing upon her. "I could take you to her room, but I shall not have time to go in with you this morning, if you will excuse me."

"Thank you, I shall do very well if you will take me to the door."

"Perhaps she is busy," Elizabeth suggested, sparring for time. "Is your business important?"

"Is she crazy?" the tall woman suddenly broke out. "She kept bothering me about her meetings and her games, but I never answered her. *I* have something to do. This morning she sent me this. Here, read it," and thus did Miss Peters's remonstrance reach the eyes for which it was intended.   It ran:

My Dear Mrs. Dowling:
I write this letter with sorrow and reluctance. I am loth to shut you out from our afternoon classes, where you might have learned something of the dignity and responsibility of motherhood.

Elizabeth glanced up at the brigadier of a woman before her and quailed. The letter continued:

For Edward's sake, too, I am sorry to ask you to discontinue your attendance, for I feel that he will learn in later years to blush for the hoydenish manner which now, perhaps, amuses him. But I am acting upon the unanimous vote of the class. We all feel that your attitude toward Mother-Play-Study-Problems is not the scientific one, and that you had better seek in some other field the enlightenment of which you stand so much in need. Or would you wish to take a course of private lessons with me?

Very truly yours,

Matilda Peters.

"Now what," demanded the brigadier, "did she mean by writing to me like that?"

"Perhaps she did n't," suggested the stricken Elizabeth.

The indignation with which this answer was received communicated itself to Edward, so that he oscillated where he stood.

"Don't I tell you that it came to me this morning?"

"But, perhaps it was not intended for you."

"Am I," the tall woman asked with almost superhuman self-control, "Edward's mother or am I not?"

"Of course, of course," Elizabeth Alvord assured her. "But perhaps some of the others ——"

"My son's other mothers! Nothing could be more likely! I presume you specialize in physiology. But I am wasting your valuable time. Where shall I find Miss Peters?"

So the mothers of Edward set out for the door of the kindergarten room — one of them was going no farther — while Edward, suspended by the clasp of his taller parent, trailed in mid-air like Aurora's torch-bearing Cupid.

And, as Elizabeth Alvord retreated toward

safety in the dim and unused fastness of the art building, Miss Peters, wild of eye and unguarded by any formulated Fröbelian principle, was glancing from a woman to a letter, from the letter to a child, and back to the woman again.   And the Expert reverted to a remote ancestral type:

"Sakes alive!" gasped Matilda Peters, A.M., Ph. G., etc. etc.   "Mercy sakes alive!"

III

USURPATION OF OFFICE

WE HAD been having all sorts of upheavals in the college. There had been stormy Faculty meetings, icy trustee meetings, vehement committee meetings and resignations by the score. Several of the most cherished of the professors had left, and the conscientious or emotional students had thereupon wept themselves into an appearance which must have "made for resignation," as Professor Guiterman would have said, on the part of the men who were going. We juniors in the Art Department were orphaned early in the epidemic when Adams resigned, and left the department without a head. It was a cruel blow to Elizabeth and to me. To her, because she rather fancied herself, like a novel heroine person, clad in a blue painting apron, being a sort of confidante and mother confessor to more reckless art students. To me, because Professor Adams's course had been less thickly set about with psychology, philosophy of education and kindred horrors than were any other of the courses leading to degrees and diplomas and intellectual pinnacles. Also, there was a large building devoted to the use of our department. And that to a person, or even to two, who much preferred "cutting" lectures to attending them is an immense advantage, and it must be admitted that we regarded our programmes as suggesting things which we might do if nothing more interesting offered rather than as cast-iron rules of life and time. Hidden in some remote drawing or modelling room, we often whiled away the hours assigned by our programmes to boredom, and vainly would Professor Adams send or even come in search of us. Two elevators and two flights of stairs made the chase a complicated up-hill and down-dale affair, and it was almost impossible to catch one — or two — who enjoyed the good will of the elevator men and the friendship of the janitor.

When Adams quarrelled with the trustees and went the way of all revolutionists we were disconsolate for some space, and full of fear. There was a rumour that we were to be assigned to other courses and professors pending the appointment of a successor to Adams. Fortunately, however, we had almost our full corps of instructors left and it was decided to let us go on under their care, with Prexy in his leisure moments acting as Adams's understudy. The chief beauty of this arrangement lay in the fact that Prexy had no leisure moments, and we found, after a week's uneasiness, that our position was improved rather than impaired. Then we cheered up sufficiently to see the sweet uses of our adversity and to adopt the deserted office suite as our own. At any other time Prexy would have discovered us, but with his Faculty resigning right and left, much faster than he could renew it, you will understand that he, poor dear, had not much time to devote to two unimportant students in their junior year.

There was an outer room filled with books and bookcases where Elizabeth used to draw, and opening off this a dear little place all filled with one big desk where I used to read and store the books most suited to my taste, and where we kept the refreshments with which we were wont to regale John and Elizabeth's many admirers at between-class repasts, when there was not time to go back to our flat. Elizabeth was always eating, and always feeding everyone she knew.

To John and to me the changes in the personnel of the Faculty were most disquieting, for they upset the regular order of precedence and promotion. Sometimes we hoped, in the event of the resignation of Professor Johnson, the head of John's department, that Prexy would give the chair to John; and at others we feared that he might appoint an outsider. There was nothing I could do to influence the course of things, but I could — and did — keep from worrying John about it, and I helped him to bear the suspense as bravely and cheerfully as it might be borne by two people to whom the outcome meant so much.

In my efforts in this regard the quiet office in the almost deserted building had been a great resource. When the work of the day was over John would cross the campus and spend a half-hour resting or talking in the big chair, and then he would let me pet him and make much of him, as he never did at any other time. In our studies, too, the room played an important part, though I think we never quite appreciated this until February brought the mid-year examinations upon our devoted and ill-informed heads.

All the halls and libraries were full of

students cramming up for the examinations. Even the clever, hardworking people waxed anxious and weary-eyed until only to look at them was to court discouragement. If Elizabeth and I had had to combat that scholastic atmosphere in our search for knowledge I fear that we should have disgraced ourselves and our instructors. But in our private office there was such an air of cheeriness that we managed to imbibe and retain sufficient store of theory and technicality. We were working hard, but we were doing well.

Wednesday afternoon was devoted to "General Method in Education." The questions were bad, but not impossible and when I had written all that I knew in answer to them, I set out to prepare tea and comfort for Elizabeth; for I inferred from the rumpling of her heavy hair, and the wrinkle between her dark eyes that things were going seriously with her. She took examinations seriously, did Elizabeth, and General Method was never a joke.

Passing through the main hall I met John, and, as no observing eye was upon us, stopped and spoke with him.

"Will you come to my office this afternoon, Marion?" said he.. "I have something to tell you."

"No, no," said I. "You come to ours. It is so much quieter. Those women students are always following you and wanting to ask you silly questions. You come to ours."

"Very well," he acquiesced. "I suppose I may as well let you enjoy it while you may. Very soon you will have to humble your pride and come to me. For you are to be evicted. They 've got a man for Adams's place. A chap I used to know at college. An awfully nice fellow, and," he added, with a cheerful laugh, "the very thing for Elizabeth." It was one of John's eccentricities to be continually looking for a sweetheart for Elizabeth; and since her advent at college he had produced an unbroken series of claimants for her hand

which embraced such diverse elements as
a widowed trustee, old and ugly and rich,
and a penniless graduate of the Philosophical
Department, who had been appointed Inspec-
tor of Schools in a damp and stagnant region
of the Philippines. It was rather as an
authority over me and my leisure than as a
suitor for my friend that the man loomed up
before me.

"When is he coming?" I asked, blankly.

"It isn't yet decided that he is coming at
all. The trustees have simply written and
asked if he would consider the position. I
hope for his own sake that he won't, unless he
is feeling peculiarly well and fit. Old Adams
had his hands full with you. But what you
must be like after two months' idleness!"

"Wrong term," said I; "spontaneous development, if you please."

As a bespectacled student, in a dark
green shirtwaist, bore down upon us, we
parted, his last words being: "I shall be
with you at five o'clock."

In keeping with Moore's theory of the
dear Gazelle which always faded away when
anybody got fond of it, the office looked
more than ever cozy and cheerful now that
there was a chance of its being taken from us.
Our books and pictures, our chafing dish,
my sewing, and Elizabeth's canary gave it
a very homelike appearance, and I set about
lighting the alcohol lamp and boiling the
kettle with a hurt and rebellious spirit.
For where else in all that heartless institution
could I sit and sew while the kettle boiled
and I waited for my own true love? And
Elizabeth! Poor old Elizabeth! I was
reflecting dismally upon these things when
the door of the outer office opened. I
could not turn to look as the kettle was
absorbing all my attention. But I called
genially: "Enjoy this glory while yet you
may, Elizabeth, for we are going to be evicted.
They have found a successor for old Adams
and, of course — selfish things men are —
he will take the office away from us."

"I should be sorry to intrude," said a grave voice, a strange voice; and a man stood in the doorway: a strange man! A grave man!

I rose suddenly from that awkward, wobbly chair, while the alcohol lamp flamed madly and the kettle boiled over. He explained that he had come to New York to look at his new quarters, students, and assistant.

"And you are?" he questioned, quite uninterestedly.

"A student," I said meekly.

"A senior?" hopefully. "You leave this term?"

"Alas, no!" I answered. I always hate to disappoint people. "A junior, and coming back next year."

He bore the situation with dignity. In fact, dignity seemed a sort of fad with him. He belonged to the stocky, stodgy, Germanesque type, which prides itself on its freedom from human characteristics. He manifested no interest, no temper, no sense of humour. And he was John's idea of an eligible *parti* for Elizabeth! For Elizabeth, tempestuous, big-hearted, beautiful. She was beautiful; even John admitted it, though never without adding: "Though I don't, of course, care for the type."

I might have rivalled the intruder's calm if I had not been unnerved by the near presence of a chocolate cake in the top drawer of the desk, and by the expectation of Elizabeth's whirlwind arrival and unmasked dismay.

"I," said he, "am Mr. Blaisdell. You say you were expecting me?"

"I," said I, "am Marion Blake. I never expected anyone less. But," I added, my manners coming once more to the fore, "I am very glad to see you." Thereupon we shook hands gravely.

"I have come," he repeated, "to look over the ground, to see the students."

"They are, unfortunately, scattered through the different examination rooms, 'suffering grinding torments,'" I quoted, thinking to lure him into a smile. But his gravity was impregnable, so I added decorously: "The building, however ——"

"Is nothing to me," he interrupted, if so leisurely a correction could be called by so energetic a name. "I am interested solely in the student body. With a group of earnest, clever young men to work with, the building and other equipment will matter very little."

Now, I think, and I have since persuaded John to think, though it took a long time, that a speech like that justified, nay even invited, the later events of that afternoon. For there was I, not earnest, not clever, and certainly not a young man. And there was he who had been asked to undertake my mental and artistic training, talking like that about young men.

For Prexy, when he sent out into the highways in search of a professor of art, was thinking quite as much of me and of Elizabeth as of young Blight, with his father's name to serve as an open sesame everywhere, or of young Grant, with his "stuff" already appearing in the magazines. Thinking even more, perhaps, of us; for we were troublesome, and most of the others were such model students that they made no ripple on the scholastic sea. Elizabeth had not yet found even one *confrère* with anything on his mind. As the padre complains in the ballade of Alice Brown:

"All the other folk in this insipid neighbourhood
  Have nothing to confess: they're so ridiculously good."

And there was, of course, no sense in our confessing to one another, for we generally planned things together, and always executed them in concert.

The introduction of Professor Blaisdell to his students-to-be was, perhaps, our masterpiece in "team work." I had volunteered to act as master of ceremonies, and he, seeing no way in which to secure a more responsible aide, accepted my services with a cold grace.

Just outside the door I was caught and comforted and purred over by Elizabeth.

"You poor darling!" she crooned. "What did he do to you? The janitor told me, but I was just too late to warn you. Was he very dreadful? Did you save the cake?"

"No," I answered dully. "It's in the top drawer of the desk with the spoons and the doilies I'm embroidering."

"And where is he?"

"Sitting at the desk: looking through it for lists of equipment and that sort of thing. Come in and be presented."

"And devoured with the cake."

"But he won't devour you. He will dislike you. He has come to inspect his students, and he wants to teach only young men."

"In a co-educational institution?" she laughed. "What impertinence!"

And suddenly the same idea occurred to both of us. If we could discourage him about his "student body" he might go away and leave us in possession of the office.

The same words hissed in both our whispers: "We 'll muster the Old Guard!"

The "Old Guard" was our name for the post-graduate body. It was recruited from all sorts of sources, but its majority was of teachers of infinite experience. Our college was peculiarly rich in this regard because its name was great in the land, so that schools, principals, and boards revered its diploma and its degrees, and paid larger salaries to such instructors as could be described in catalogues as having been trained by us. So there came out of the West, and South, and East men and women ready to sacrifice everything to ambition. Ready to live meagrely and to work unendingly for the right to tack to their names A. M.'s, Ph. D.'s, or D. S.'s. They were utterly regardless of health, pleasure, or leisure, and, stripped of the distinction attaching to the position of "teacher" on their native heaths, they were a pathetic and puzzling problem to our Faculty, and a horrible warning to younger students just entering the profession which, of all others, is most ungrateful to its workers. They were hard to find that day owing to the examinations, but finally, up in the water-colour room, we discovered Mrs. Magrotty, an "Old Guard" of a somewhat different type. She was a large, stout, black-serge widow, and she was taking up art because her grandson — aged eight — had shown remarkable aptitude for drawing cats, and she considered him destined to be an artist, and wanted to work with him at home, distrusting the "studio atmosphere" for the young.

When she heard our tidings she got into a wonderful flurry. She took off her glasses, patted the prim gray puffs upon her brow, and shook the black serge into its proper folds.

"And have you seen him?" she asked us.

"Marion has," answered Elizabeth. "And does n't like him. She 's the only one who has spoken to him."

She was a large, stout, black-serge widow

"Most unfortunate beginning," Mrs. Magrotty muttered, as we led her to the elevator. "Quite an erroneous impression. Not at all a type of our students. I'm glad you came to me." Doubtless she meant to be nasty, but I could have pressed the black serge to my grateful breast if my arms had been longer or the serge less vast.

"You take her in," Elizabeth whispered, tilting Mrs. Magrotty's mortar-board at a disgraceful angle upon her venerable head. "I'll go and drum up the others" — and she did. She knows now, and bitterly bewails, that she missed the greatest treat of our two-year course when she absented herself from those introductions. Mr. Blaisdell must have been exploring while I was away, for there was a heap of my books on the desk, the third drawer was slightly open, and there was a gloomy stiffness in the air which struck cold to the soles of my feet. He looked up at us as we came in with an aloofness, an impersonal regard, a boredom which staggered me for a moment, and then made me hotly angry. Mrs. Magrotty was blandly beaming, and I went through the introduction.

"Mr. Blaisdell," I began, "may I present you to Mrs. Magrotty, a student in the sophomore year in this department." He winced as I had hoped he would, when he realized what was before him, but his manners were perfect. With absolute impassiveness he bowed before her spreading smile and accepted her grimy hand.

"Professor," she began, in the surprisingly high voice which some very stout people have, "it is a great relief to have you with us; a great relief." Again he bowed. "You were needed," she squeaked on. "Very badly needed, I regret to say, by some of us," and she looked chidingly at me.

Again he turned those eyes of his on me, and I, to my everlasting surprise and wrath, blushed scarlet. At which he looked more bored than ever.

"Indeed, yes," I broke in; "Mrs. Magrotty has so much wanted an adviser. She can find no really good authority on the proper age at which she'd better allow her grandson to take up perspective."

"Her grandson!" he repeated.   "Her grandson! I understood that Mrs. Magrotty was herself the student."

"Why, so I am!" she cried.   "But, Professor, I have a life work, a sacred trust from the grave."

"A grandson?" he suggested.

"A sweet child," I gurgled, with my eyes on the ceiling. I had hardly hoped to start her so easily, but in a second she was off. She told him the whole story, disease, last words, baby talk, family secrets, habits of father — all. He listened gravely, but without any vehement sympathy, and, as she babbled on, he solemnly joined his hands, finger by finger. Simultaneously his eyes and mine fell upon a large brown smudge upon his irreproachable cuff. Chocolate! I

faded into the outer office and there I found
Elizabeth. She had bagged two more victims, Miss Perkins and Miss Jones. "Take
them in!" she cried, "I'll get another,"
and was gone.

Miss Perkins was the most coy and fluttering person I have ever seen. She brought
a large and well-charged palette with her.
In her childish excitement at Elizabeth's
urgent summons she had forgotten to discard it or the brown denim apron which
shielded her tall slimness. She had taught
sewing in all the really important church
schools of Loper, Cavalier County, North
Dakota, for the last fifteen years, but her
ambition soared to higher things, her soul
hungered for a broader life, and it became
my pleasant duty to introduce her to Professor Blaisdell. I did it in a speech, a lubri-
cating little speech, but he seemed too com-
pletely absorbed in his newest charge to
hear me. And really she had the gentlest
face — and the stupidest — of which the col-

lege boasted. She fluttered and sighed and dropped her eyes, and the large palette — butter side down, of course — bashfully, when he arose to his bulky proportions before her. The palette fell upon his neat shoe, and he said a word which made Mrs. Magrotty more than ever sure that the home was the best place for sacred charges.

Miss Jones went off rather better. Miss Oliver stared more than a lady and a teacher should, and said less. Miss Moore balked at first sight, and had to be literally run in by the master of ceremonies. By this time the meeting had reached such proportions that it was adjourned to the outer office, much to my relief and to Elizabeth's uneasiness when she heard that he was now sitting at her table.

Finally she reported that there was not another unpresentable art student on the grounds. She had collected a dozen and could find no more. So I dragged her in, and watched him closely as his tired eyes rested on her. He had looked coldly, it is true, upon me — a thing quite new to my experience — but I certainly expected some lightening of his gloom when he should look upon Elizabeth. But there was no glint of interest in his clever face.

So we all sat stiffly along the wall, and he made us a little address. It was neat and cold, like a biscuit tortoni, and it told us about self-activity and the work of the teacher in society; his weight as an official and as a man. At that word Elizabeth exclaimed:

"There! I knew I'd forget somebody, and I did!"

Even an interruption could not disturb our professor. He was still miles away as he asked:

"You have forgotten?"

"Our Fellow," cried Elizabeth. Perhaps his bushy eyebrows did contract slightly at this frank avowal of mormonism. Perhaps the one emotion of which he was capable, as he glanced from one to another of his

We all sat stiffly along the wall, and he made us a little address

future charges, was pity for the man they claimed in common.

"May I ask you to explain?" said he. "Your — fellow — did you say?" And Mrs. Magrotty sprang to his instruction.

"Why, yes!" she cried, "we've got a Fellow."

"Only one?" he asked politely; though it was plain to see that he quite believed it. "One among so many?"

"The trustees don't seem to care to give more. You'll see about him in the catalogue," said Mrs. Magrotty, while I found a catalogue and the place and pointed to the legend:

"The McClaren Fellowship in Applied Art awarded to Herbert Maimer."

"Oh!" said he in a tone which explained everything, and Elizabeth rocked with unregenerate glee. "Oh!" said he again, and looked up at me so quickly that he caught a beatified grin in transit, and was hardly impressed by the deferential gloom with which I replaced it.

"And where," he asked courteously, "where, Miss Blake, is your Fellow?"

Of course I did n't know. I never did fancy him. Neither did Elizabeth. But he seemed to fit into Miss Perkins's idea of "the broader life," and Mrs. Magrotty had quite adopted him. It was grandmother who now interposed with:

"He is making casts in the modelling room. I can't think the work is good for him. There is so much danger of inhaling the plaster of Paris."

"I'll fetch him!" cried Elizabeth in a little spurt. The upper half of the door was muffled glass, and it was certainly thoughtless of Elizabeth to go into kinks of laughter just outside it. Then she collected her energies and vanished, and a heavy pause followed. Mr. Blaisdell read the catalogue's version of our Fellow's biography and seemed to be less impressed than ever. He stared moodily and absently at Miss Perkins until she felt called upon to speak.

She always spoke most when she was most embarrassed.

"Mr. Maimer," she began, and blushed scarlet, "Mr. Maimer has a very fine mind."

"Truly?" said Mr. Blaisdell, while Miss Oliver stared at him.

"Yes," Mrs. Magrotty broke in. "He has a fine personality. So inspiring!"

"And he is working out his thesis now," Mrs. Magrotty went on. "He discusses it with me. I am a grandmother, and of course I can help him in some ways. His topic is: 'The Hand and Its Relation to Beauty in the Home.' It's a privilege to work with such a thought."

"And with such a man," purred Miss Perkins.

"Truly?" said Mr. Blaisdell, while Miss Oliver stared at him. Nothing else of moment occurred, except the sudden and unexplained up-flaring of the electric lights, before Elizabeth returned with our Fellow. There we were all sitting stiffly in the early dark of a

February afternoon, feeling ill at ease and somewhat rebellious in the antagonistic presence of the new man. Suddenly the lights sprang out, and we were looking blinkingly at the new man and he was looking unblinkingly at us. And surely Elizabeth had done her work well. To a man who wanted a class of clever, earnest young men the collection of dowagers before him must have been upsetting. His feelings were too deep for silence and they forced him to speak to me.

"And are these, Miss Blake, all the students?"

"Not all," I admitted; "but representative. Mrs. Judkins is absent because her daughter had chicken pox, and Miss Ackerson's rheumatism ——"

"Are there any male students?"

"Of course, Miss Alvord has gone for him." And then the door opened and Elizabeth came in with Mr. Maimer.

"Look at him!" she besought me, superfluously, for no one could have avoided doing it. "His apron string is tied in a black, black knot, and will you look at his face?"

Mrs. Magrotty's fears had been well-founded. The modelling room had not agreed with Mr. Maimer. His golden hair stood wildly erect upon his head, his collar hung dejectedly about his neck; his butcher's apron emphasized his diminutive proportions, and his face was whitened like a clown's.

Professor Blaisdell glanced from the harem to Mr. Maimer, and from Mr. Maimer back to the harem. I was overcome by emotion and it was Elizabeth, radiantly smiling, who did the presentation. Some one found a knife and disembarrassed the Fellow of his apron, and the opening remarks were resumed as soon as the "inspiring personality" was disposed between Mrs. Morgan and Miss Perkins.

Professor Blaisdell resumed. It was a beautiful talk, and it made me wonder what

I should ever do with the "responsibility of the teacher," if it — and a degree — should become mine. Also I was wondering how we should get Blaisdell safely off the premises without encountering any more promising students when again the door opened and John came in. If anything could have reconciled me to Blaisdell it would have been his evident pleasure at the sight of John and John's evident pleasure at sight of him.

During the greetings the student body trailed itself away. Elizabeth and I retreated into the inner office, and the two friends were left alone.

"I wish," said John, "that I had known you were here this afternoon. I should have arranged a meeting between you and your future students."

"I've met enough of them, thank you," the other replied grimly.

"You're not to be discouraged by the old ladies who were here when I came in,"

John urged. "They are perfectly harmless and well-meaning, and they give very little trouble. I have several in my department. But I 'm talking about your young fellows — and even a few of the girls. You 'll have some of the best raw material in the college to work with. Splendid, earnest youngsters. Wait till you see them."

"I have met two of the young women," Blaisdell remarked. "Miss Blake and Miss Alvord were so kind as to constitute themselves sponsors for this afternoon's introductions."

I clutched Elizabeth, and waited for John's next words:

"Ah, yes!" said my own true love in a carefully casual voice. "What did you think of them ?"

"I thought them," said John's latest claimant for Elizabeth's hand, "I thought them perhaps the most utterly objectionable young persons I had ever met. If I should decide to accept this position I foresee great difficulty with them and for them. That Miss Blake seems especially undisciplined and spoiled. I 've never, in all my experience, met a student quite like her."

"No," John acquiesced, blandly, while Elizabeth chuckled, "neither, do you know, have I."

IV

EVE AND THE ORANGE

THE summer which separated my last two
college years was the very happiest
summer I had ever known. Mother and I
took a camp in one of those semi-literary,
semi-artistic settlements which do so much
to make the North Woods possible for the
timid and the unattached female. Not that
we were by any means unattached. But
if we had been so, the principle would have
been the same. The place was wonderful
beyond compare: the people were charming,
and the weather was unquestionable.

We had been introduced and vouched for
by a charter member of the settlement, and
from the day of our arrival we were made
welcome and comfortable. But when it was
discovered that I was the fiancée of "that

amazing young chap, Wentworth" of our college, I became immediately a personage. And, later, when this same Professor Wentworth finished his course of lectures at the Summer School and joined us for rest and recreation, it seemed to me that I was too happy, that such perfect content could not last. Everyone pretended utter unconsciousness of our emotional states, and yet there was not one in all that romantic, Forest of Arden company who did not plan and contrive that John and I should have endless and uninterrupted opportunities for the enjoyment of our own society. It was reassuring to me, and I hope it was so to John to find how beautifully we got on together. For he was a learned professor — a professor of philosophy — while I was only a somewhat idle, somewhat frivolous student in his college. It will always be a comfort to me to know that John knew these little characteristics of mine before he knew much else about me. They cannot surprise him now.

There was never a jarring note in all the perfect days. Even rain was pleasant and companionable, and quite without the vindictiveness which it shows in town. We were happy, and we were busy — John with a text book which he had undertaken to prepare, and I with trousseau embroidery or with libellous water-colour sketches of our favourite haunts. He was good enough to say that I was of infinite help to him, that if he succeeded in setting down a theory in words which I could understand, then he was quite sure that he had made his meaning very clear indeed. He used to be really triumphant about it with a simplicity at which no one could have taken offence, though I suppose it was not exactly complimentary to what Matthew Arnold would call my "openness of mind and flexibility of intelligence." And I used to be wild with pride when he would recognize or identify my pictures. He did so rarely.

We never talked of college. "Conversational Rule No. 1," as by John set down, read: "No shop." Even the most casual or accidental mention of our classic halls was punishable by our law, and the party of the other part could exact a heavy fine. And yet, one blessed afternoon, when I was paddling lazily, and John was trolling still more lazily, he deliberately broke the rule.

"I had a letter," he announced, "from President Arnott."

"You will pay for this," I threatened.

"When we reach shore," he pleaded. "It's so unsafe to move about in a canoe, and in clear view of Mother Carey's cottage." He called our nearest neighbour that, for no more reasonable reason than that she kept chickens. "And perhaps you will withhold sentence when you hear the news he sent me."

"Is it about the Art Department?" I asked.

"All about it," John laughed. "Blaisdell has accepted the position of director.

He 'll make you work as you have never worked before. You might write and warn Elizabeth Alvord."

"But this is dreadful, truly dreadful. Does all the work we did that afternoon, Elizabeth and I, count for nothing?"

"Hardly that, I should think," he cheered me. "Blaisdell has a most retentive memory, and it was a brilliant performance. He will not forget his first meeting with you."

The worst thing that could happen to me and to Elizabeth was that Professor Blaisdell should not forget his first meeting with us. We had counted upon his refusing the position with contumely and scorn.

Yet he had done nothing of the kind. He would be there to inflict daily tortures upon us, and the happy paths of idleness and joy would no longer echo to our tread. Whenever I thought of what lay before me I, too, broke Conversational Rule No. 1 and made John tell me about this Professor Blaisdell, who had been at college with him, and with whom he had kept up ever since one of those pleasant, casual, inarticulate sorts of friendships so common among men and so unknown among women. But nothing that I heard reassured me, and I did *not* write to Elizabeth. Which, under the circumstances, showed remarkable self-control.

I was forced to tell her the day before the opening of the fall term, when she, Margaret and I foregathered in our little flat. I found her there wrestling with trunks and breathless with exertion and curiosity when I arrived. When the first rush of greeting was over, when we had exchanged views of new gowns and news of old friends, Elizabeth pounced upon me with the questions I had been dreading.

"Yes," I answered, "he has accepted."

"Not really?" she gasped.

"Very really."

She bore it badly. More badly, I think, than I had done. She stormed and she . laughed; she raged and she pranced; she jumped and she thumped; she behaved just as the Mariner does in the "Just So Stories," when he finds himself in the whale's dark inside cupboards. And in good sooth it was a serious thing for us. A professor can do much to make smooth or rough the ways of the students, and we had forfeited all title to this man's consideration. Oh! yes, and in very truth, we were in for it.

We were. We agreed to try him with one propitiatory remark, and to determine our future course by his response. Elizabeth tried first, and he did not respond at all. She said she was glad; that the year seemed more bearable, somehow, when she could look forward to some little excitement every day.

"And I think, Marion," she told me, "that he hardly understands what is before him. I feel exactly as Marmion did when Douglas was so rude about shaking hands. You remember?" And lest I should not, she proceeded to recite the lines with such feeling that Margaret emerged from the

kitchen in agitated tears, to report that she
would n't be answerable for the dinner if
Miss Elizabeth kep' up them theayter pieces.
She vanished with incredible dexterity when
she received the full force of the lines:

> " And if thou say'st I am not peer
> To any lord in Scotland here,
> Highland or lowland, far or near,
> Lord Angus, thou hast *lied.* "

Elizabeth delivered this defiance with such
vigour and looked so pretty and foolish when
Margaret had retreated with a howl, that I
knew she had been believing that Blaisdell
himself was before her.

I fared somewhat better with my pen-
ance, though I wonder if John knows what
it cost me to eat humble pie; to watch Elizabeth's skirmishes and battles and to take
no active part in them. I was constantly
thinking of the most outrageous things to
do and say, and as constantly restraining
myself with the reflection that the man was
a friend of my dear's, and that it behooved

me to prepare his mind to receive, without too much astonishment, the news of our engagement when the time for its announcement should come. Even to be engaged is a little trammelling. I wonder what the Faculty wives will think of me when I am really one of them. I can't imagine what it will be like.

It took about a month for the report of the very uncordial relations existing between Professor Blaisdell and Elizabeth Alvord to reach the other members of the Faculty, and after that his life was made hideous about it. There was never a Faculty meeting or a Faculty dinner at which he was not reminded of his fair failure. For Elizabeth was undeniably lovely, one of the beauties of the college. She was immensely popular, too, with such of the professors as had never tried to teach her anything. She was always gay, always entertaining, always ready with a joke or a funny story, and she never by any chance wanted to talk shop. . When the

Students' Club gave a tea she was always well in the forefront of the receiving committee. When a new student arrived, she was sent for by Prexy, and that student was entrusted to her care. When a girl fell ill, it was always Elizabeth who went to see her, who brought her books, who would even, if the student's earnestness demanded it, attend alien lectures and report them to the invalid. On these occasions she would take notes with a brilliancy and a grasp which would have made many an eager learner green with envy. But she always interpolated little personal remarks — the colour of the professor's necktie, the progress of his cold, the rate at which Miss Perkins stared at him, the point at which Mr. Maimer fell asleep, and the word which Miss Jones said when her fountain pen ran dry. All these things she would set carefully down, and she was quite capable of handing a report, thus decorated, to the professor who gave the lecture. You will easily see that these little characteristics, though agreeable

enough in themselves, were not calculated
to endear her to a man like Blaisdell.   He
generally accepted her remarks with a weary
patience, and answered them with a silent
inclination of his heavy head, though I sometimes thought I saw a flash of something
which, in a more human being, might have
been what scientific books call "the dawn
of apperception."

Week after week went by.   The Art Department fell into step and marched steadily
toward the Christmas holidays, and the spirit
of the new professor did its good and perfect
work. No one was ever late, except Miss
Alvord. No one ever "cut" a lecture or a
drawing hour, except Miss Alvord. No one
ever answered the professor's Socratic questions with a conversational "I wonder now,"
or "I 've never looked into the matter," or
"What is your own theory? You 've formed
one, surely," except always Miss Alvord.

She was ever just short of open rudeness,
or open rebellion, and she had a way of

carelessly supplying the correct answer often enough to keep her standing on the books. But she never answered eagerly, proudly, as the other hypnotized students did. She always chose a difficult question, and she would produce the explanation in a detached, uninterested way, as though she had found it on the floor, declined to be responsible for it, but submitted it as an interesting object.

Then for some days she would play the rôle of Puck, and turn the well-ordered studios into pandemonium. One morning Mrs. Magrotty hauled her drawing bench and board to their accustomed place, rubbed her glasses, adjusted them carefully, stared at the empty shelf before her, orientated herself by the casts and pictures round about, and then broke into a shrill:

"Why, Professor! Professor Blaisdell! Do step here a moment. Some one has eaten my model."

"Eaten your model?" repeated Blaisdell, while Elizabeth, in unseemly mirth, doubled over her board. "Eaten your model, did you say?"

"Why, yes," maintained Grandmother Magrotty, "eaten it all, and left nothing but the core."

And Elizabeth's only explanation was that she liked apples, and adored grapes. She was not in the least embarrassed, but I think Mr. Blaisdell was as he glowered at her. There are punishments prescribed for her offence, but she had rather outgrown them, he sadly realized.

She never did outgrow her healthy young appetite, and I often thought it was that which so endeared her to our Margaret. She could eat anything at any time, and the fair smoothness of her complexion, the radiant health which never failed her, spoke volumes for the power of her digestion. So did Margaret, insistently. She loved John, also on account of his capacity, and to him would she make her moan:

"That poor little crabbathawn o' yours

gets no good of the little bit she picks. Not enough to keep the life in a bird has passed her lips this day, an' me makin' an' mixin' to try could I tempt her. If she was mine, as she is yours, I'd be in dread she was marked for a decline."

In vain I protested; in vain I referred to my quite satisfactory weight. Margaret's parting slap was always the same:

"Look at Miss Elizabeth, now; she'd eat all before her an' bloom like a rose. If that one runs short of wittles it's my belief she'd eat whatever came to her hand and thrive on it."

"Of course I should," Elizabeth would laugh; "I'd find food on a desert island. I just wish I was cast away on one." And superstitious people might think that she brought her adventure upon herself by tempting the fates like that.

The adventure originated, innocently and remotely enough, in the donation of a collection of marbles, newly discovered in a Grecian island, to the Museum of Art. Now the curator of the museum was a friend of our professor's, and Blaisdell was granted a private audience with the foreign ladies and gentlemen, or with such portions of them as had survived the centuries. He found them charming. I suppose their perfect calm and poise appealed to him. And he secured his friend's permission to convoy his students to see them, before the public should be admitted to that wing of the museum in which they were embowered, amid tropic verdure — borrowed for the formal opening from the Horticultural Hall — so that the beholder could form some idea of their appearance in classic days and groves.

Now, whenever Professor Blaisdell thought of his class, he thought of its fifteen or twenty young men and its ten or twelve young women who were really talented, and to whose teaching and advancement he devoted all his energies. It was his graceful habit to ignore the post-graduates and to disregard the flippant youngsters — Elizabeth and me, for example — who were taking the art course because it was easier than any of the others. There was no one to warn him that several of his predecessors had steered several excursions to different quagmires of boredom and discomfort, and that his younger students were bound by a horrible oath to attend no more of them. Only among the postgraduates, hungry for Eastern Culture, was the peripatetic method of education tolerated. And on the day set apart for the Grecian sculptures, only three undergraduates rallied to the call: Elizabeth, because she wished to see Blaisdell writhing among the postgraduates; young Blight, because he scented an opportunity for confidential speech with Elizabeth; and I, because of a disagreeable sense of responsibility for John's friend and my own.

Elizabeth gained her object promptly. The professor began to writhe immediately upon seeing the serried ranks awaiting him on the campus, and I was aware that, for a second's space, the excursion hung in the balance. But duty, and his own desire to look again upon the marbles, conquered our leader's indecision, and presently the cavalcade set out.

Some days in their earliest dawn are marked for failure, and this was one of them for Professor Blaisdell. Even the weather betrayed that conscientious educator, and drizzled miserably as we made our way to the nearest line of trolleys. You know how many different agitations beset the timid, middle-aged traveller. How she loses her purse, and then discovers it in the deepest dark of her Boston bag. How she draws out her handkerchief, and a shower of peppermint drops follows; how she trips up the conductor with her umbrella and then entangles it in her neighbour's millinery; how in dozens of different ways she is miserable, distraught, and flustered. All these vicissitudes and many more overtook Professor Blaisdell's charges, and in each of them he was appealed to, until his temper, never of the best, seethed beneath his correct frock coat.

We reached the Museum wet, miserable, and bedraggled. There was a further series of *contretemps* in the vestibule, when the doorkeeper inexorably tore umbrellas, Boston bags, box lunches, and rubbers from the students, and when the amazed curator underwent a hasty introduction and a fire of questions. The Museum is always a beautiful and inspiring place, but on that day it was a veritable fairyland. Palms and ferns were everywhere, and the statues shone among them like the gods and goddesses they were. And the wide marble staircase was banked with orange trees bearing, after the wonderful manner of their kind, bud and leaf and flower and fruit. Elizabeth marked the latter with a cheering eye, and I think she was daring young Blight to get one for her — Eve to the life! When we had wandered to our hearts' content among the new marbles, some one proposed that, being in the Museum, we ought to go through it thoroughly — it was one means to Eastern culture — and the professor, with the air of resignation which so especially exasperated Elizabeth, languidly agreed to act as cicerone.   It was, I think, at about this time that I first missed Elizabeth, but I was so busy keeping Mrs. Magrotty quiet and preventing her expressing to Blaisdell her opinion of the *altogethers* about us, that I had no time to run my friend to earth and to protect the decorations.   Besides which, I sympathized perfectly with her boredom, and knew that if I had been fancy free I should have chosen, even as she had, to wander off with young Blight instead of being herded from room to room with a lot of steaming, mackintoshed females.   When at last it was over, and we halted at the big front door, Professor Blaisdell counted his charges and discovered that two were missing.

"Where is Miss Alvord?" he said, holding me responsible, as everyone did, for the eccentricities of Elizabeth, and I could only answer hopefully, yet apologetically, that I thought she must have been tired and that we should find her at the college.

But she was not there, and, though I waited about until six o'clock, she did not come. Young Blight, however, turned up, and reported that she had left him to rejoin us early in the afternoon, when he had stolen away to visit some friend of a later vintage than those among the ferns and palms. Then I began to grow uneasy, for, with all her faults, Elizabeth is a darling, and, with all her spirit, she is not the sort of girl to do anything really unmaidenly or rash. I hurried to the apartment, but she was not there. We waited half an hour for her to come to dinner, but she did not come. Then I rang up John, who was as blessedly re-assuring as he always is. By this time old Margaret was in tears and my dinner was a most uncomfortable one. Its climax was a frightfully burned apple pie, and I was wondering whether to do violence to Margaret's feelings or my own constitution when John arrived. He affected to treat Elizabeth's disappearance lightly, but I knew him well enough to see that it was beginning to trouble him. It was by that time half after seven, and quite dark.

"There is only one thing to do," said he, when another half hour had gone uneventfully by. "We'll ring up Blaisdell and get him here. He must learn not to scatter maidens about his path. He took her out; he must be made to bring her back."

I had no great confidence in Professor Blaisdell's interest nor in his power, but John blithely summoned him from his apartment, and he was presently vowing that no power in heaven or earth — or any other place — would induce him to conduct another excursion. It was worse, he vowed, than a fresh air fund outing, and he would be antecedently condemned if he had ever before heard of people—adults, he called them—who were foolish enough to get lost in a simple little trip of a few hours' duration.

"That's all very well," John reassured him. "Nobody wants you to conduct another excursion. We only insist that you finish the one you began, and find the sweet young lady who went so blithely and confidently forth into the world with you, and whom you heartlessly abandoned."

And then John began to discourse upon the charms of Elizabeth, and I began to help him. But our words were as nothing to the woe and lamentations of Margaret. She soon identified the ponderous stranger, who seemed to take up all the cubic feet in our miniature *salon*, as the guide who had abandoned her darling, and she had given vent to a surprising amount of feeling before I could get her comfortably shut into the kitchen. I kept her there only by reminding her how hungry our poor lost one would be when she should be restored to us.

We thought and puzzled and thought,

but we could get no further than the fear and the hope that Elizabeth had been left in the Museum. Professor Blaisdell, looking like a man convicted of the blackest crime, finally determined to go back to the classic groves and look for her. He rang up his friend the curator, and found that the doors had been locked immediately after our departure, and would not be open again till nine o'clock the following morning.

"I should like to return there this evening," we heard Blaisdell say. "I — ah — mislaid — something this afternoon. Yes, I should wish to go to-night. Immediately, if you can arrange it so. Yes, of considerable value. Oh! no, not a watch; nothing like that. The article is valuable mainly for its associations" — "I should not wish," he explained to us, "to let my friend know that I lost a young lady. It might strike him as being, ah — unusual — to say the least."

"So it might," John acquiesced. I was speechless.

Finally Blaisdell hung up the receiver and turned to us. "Miss Blake," said he, "I hope you will find it convenient to accompany me. The watchman at the Museum has orders to admit us on the presentation of my card; and you, Wentworth," he went on, turning to John, "you won't desert us?"

"Oh! no," said John, "I 'll uphold you; but when you next take your little ones out for the day, you had better tie blue ribbons to their necks and lead them. This 'Little-Bo-Peep-has-lost-her-sheep' attitude seems hardly natural in you."

It was only by the exercise of great tact and strength that we separated Margaret from her bonnet and shawl and dissuaded her from accompanying the relief expedition, and as we were waiting in the outer hall for the slow-climbing elevator, she dashed, or rather lunged out upon us and forced a tissue-wrapped bundle into Professor Blaisdell's breast pocket.

" 'T is a sangwich for the lamb," she

rumbled. " 'T will stay her till I get the feeding of her again."

I was dreadfully uneasy about Elizabeth, but I was assured that she would be found now that John had undertaken to find her; and even Professor Blaisdell began to be interested, and to lay out plans and to discuss what had better be done if our quest should prove unwarranted, and we did not find the child in the museum. The watchman had his orders, and supplied us with little electric searchlights, with which we, went flashing through the building like three giant fireflies. Professor Blaisdell soon wandered away from us, and John and I were left among the orange trees.

"What will he do when he finds her?" I asked, after some more personal conversation. "Do you think he will scold her?"

"I have been wondering, too," he answered. "He is really, you know, a very fine fellow, though neither you nor she believes it. I wish I could be watching."

"Oh! so do I," I breathed, "but of course we can't."

And yet, after all, we were. We found her first. Poor little Raven Locks, asleep on a bench, with her hat off, her coat rolled into a pillow for her tired head, and orange peels radiating all about her on the floor. Such a pathetic, forlorn, "Alas, I have no one to love me" little figure, with her heavy hair half loose, and her cheeks flushed with crying. She has always denied the crying, but when John turned his searchlight on her face her eyelashes were wet. And I don't see why she was not entitled to any amount of tears. It was a horrible situation in which to find herself. Locked into that great, dark building, all hungry and tired and lonely as she was. I was just about to touch her when John caught my hand.

"Let him find her," he suggested. "You and I can watch."

So we crept behind a person sans head, sans legs, sans arms, sans everything, and waited. Elizabeth, with the whimsical fancy which never deserted her, had chosen to go to sleep beside the statue of the poor little Babes in the Wood, and there she lay, as helpless and as pretty as the marble children beside her. And there the professor, flickering toward her like a searchlight gone mad, found his valuable article. For some seconds he was perfectly quiet. But the light played over Elizabeth, rested on the gloom of her hair and the fairness of her face, thrown into such brilliant relief by her pillow of Persian lamb and lynx. Then it crept up to the statue, then down to the orange peels, then back again to her. And she was lying just as the little sculptured girl lay, with one hand under her cheek, and the other, open palm upward, beside her. For a long time he studied her face and watched her gentle breathing. And no wonder he was surprised. He had never seen her without the light of mischief and mockery in her eyes. With him she was always on her guard, always defiant, hard, and brilliant. No wonder he found it hard to recognize this pink and white lovely girl child, gathered into a sad little heap in the corner of a bench. She looked half her size, and a quarter her age. Then he stooped and touched her hair; put one heavy wave, which had fallen across her cheek, back. I hardly breathed, for even I, to whom Elizabeth was so accustomed, cannot touch her without awakening her, and yet she slept serenely on.

Stooping so he caught sight of the tears on her eyelashes; he seemed more bewildered and more upset than ever. He caught his breath sharply, and Elizabeth stirred. Instantly all was dark again, and John and I, crouching behind the statue, were beginning to think he had lost the combination of his lamp. It was very weird and eerie to wait in that great, dark hall, with enormous statues looming around us, and to hear nothing except our own breathing and the faint, far-away clang of a trolley car. And then, just as I felt the silence unendurable, Pro-

fessor Blaisdell turned on his lamp again
and touched Elizabeth authoritatively on the
shoulder. In the first instant of her awakening she beamed, absolutely beamed upon her
enemy. She explained afterward that she
had forgotten there was such a thing as an
enemy in the world. So for the moment
Blaisdell was only somebody she knew, and
she was radiantly, dangerously glad to see him,
and Elizabeth dangerously radiant is not to
be ignored. So he shook hands with her
inanely, and then produced Margaret's mes-
sage before she was quite awake. When
she saw the tissue paper and the fringed
napkin she nearly, or I imagined it, threw
herself upon his broad chest, and she was in
a whirlwind of chicken mayonnaise sandwich,
and Professor Blaisdell was urging her to
caution, when John and I bore down upon
them. Presently we went out into the night, .
past the bewildered watchman, who saw four
go out where he had seen but three go in.
Altogether the events of that night might

have puzzled the management, for, as I passed the orange trees upon the stairs, "I marked with one eye," as the Lobster says, that they bore, according to generous habit of their kind, leaf and bud and blossom. But no fruit. And even to this day Elizabeth's dauntless appetite balks at the merest flavour of oranges.

"For they were the cause of all the trouble," she explained, late on that historic night. "I wanted one off those foolish trees — wanted to see if they were real — and I had to wait so long to let everyone out of the way that I was caught. I shall never forgive Billy Blight. I asked him to get me one. And later I ate dozens of them. They *were* real — and nasty. As decorations they 're beautiful, but as a diet!"

"You found what you lost, sir?" the watchman accosted Blaisdell respectfully.

"Thank you, I did!" answered the Professor, parting with a tip which made the watchman more than ever sure that he was suffering from a multiplying vision.

"Ah! sir," he went on, "them big buildings is treacherous places to lose your valuables in. It's not everyone that finds them again. You're very lucky."

"I am," said Blaisdell. "I'm sensible of that."

Yet John and I knew that for the second time in one day the professor had lost something at the Museum of Art.

"Oh, my gracious!" cried Elizabeth, clutching my arm as we moved off under the trees. "I suppose I'm done for now, Marion. This is the worst thing I ever did. He'll never get over this night."

"Ah, well," said I, noting that there was certainly no animosity in Blaisdell's face; "I should n't despair if I were you."

V

BILLY BLIGHT

JOHN and I frequently agreed — it was a subject which we often discussed — that the only thing which kept Billy Blight and Elizabeth Alvord from rushing into one another's arms and being happy ever after was their blatant suitability for one another. Even John admitted that Billy possessed ten qualifications to one of Blaisdell's; and yet our beauty ignored young Lochinvar and tried to live up to Blaisdell's impossible standards.

Elizabeth and Billy were both young, both good to look upon, both of independent means and independent spirit. There was no one in the least like either of them, except, of course, the other; but throughout the greater part of our stay at college these two

young people treated each other in the most
casual way possible. If they, by some infre-
quent chance, walked or talked together —
he so fair and tall and strong; she so dark
and slim — there were always emotional
students to watch them and to gush of the
mediæval knights and ladies who had lent
splendour to the Table Round. For Romance raises its head in most unlikely
places, and many a worn out woman, who
has spent her life in teaching the three
R's and destroying her nervous system,
will yet join with all the world in love
of a lover. But Billy and Elizabeth,
made up, dressed and cast for the rôles of
jeune premier and *ingenue*, allowed act after
act of the play to go by without reaching
that understanding which the audience felt
entitled to expect from them.

Their being at our college at all savoured
of the preordained. We were an earnest,
humdrum, studious lot, as was but natural
in an institution whose object was the rather

humdrum and prosaic one of training teachers. That we were co-educational did very little to enliven us, for the majority of the men students, "Eds," we used to call them, were post-graduates, serious, bespectacled, and uninteresting. Against this background of masculine mediocrity Billy Blight glowed like a kingfisher in a leafless thicket.

Hardly less conspicuous was Elizabeth among the women. She was always so beautifully dressed and perfectly turned out from head to foot that without suggesting fashion plates she yet radiated fashion and grace. It may be mentioned in all loving kindness and sincere appreciation that the majority of us were inclined to dowdiness. I suppose it *is* discouraging to dress oneself for a great number of years for the approbation of no one in particular.

"My dear Marion," John would remark, "we simply *must* marry Elizabeth; you and she have always been together, and you can't very well now return her to her bachelor uncles."

"She'd upset their correct establishment in a week," I interpolated.

"We can't leave her entirely to Margaret's care. A girl like Elizabeth requires something more sophisticated in the way of a duenna if she's going to set up an establishment of her own."

"I suppose she *is* too pretty for that," I agreed.

"And too mischievous," said John. "Too wild. Too spoiled. I know she's never got into a serious scrape yet, but that's only a question of time. The Faculty is not always so entertained as she means it to be by her little outbreaks and insubordinations. If it weren't for her plausibility and her irresistible affectation of being as seriously surprised and annoyed by herself as any one of us could be, she would have been expelled long ago."

"Expelled!" said I, with proper indignation, "you know perfectly well that she is far and away the cleverest, best read, and best liked student in the college. And she's popular, too, with both the Faculty and the students. You would n't dare to expel her just for being high-spirited, and no one can ever accuse her of being anything more."

"She's all that you say," said John. "Nevertheless, an irate Faculty sets low value on high spirits, and I want to get her off your conscience before you and I are married. I admire and like her as well as anybody does, but I think she'd be very much in the way of 'love in a cottage'; but it may come to that, if we can't get anyone to take her off our hands."

This was to me a new and rather serious view of the situation, and yet I could n't help loving John for his conscientiousness; though I was rather determined that he'd have no reason to exercise it.

When Elizabeth at last began to "see" Billy it was not at all through the nimbus of sentiment. She came home one day to lunch in her cap and gown, though we seldom left the campus in our academic garb. Still, our apartment was distant no more than a block and a half from the gates, and when a lecturer ran over time or when we loitered about afterward, we thought nothing of traversing that quiet bit of street just as we were instead of going down to subterranean lockers to change. Now I, too, had been at the lecture, and I knew that Professor Blaisdell had not run over his time. And so I knew that loitering must be the explanation.

"I was talking to young Blight," she announced, without any encouraging embarrassment. "He seems to be ever so good-natured a fellow."

"He is; he does," I acquiesced somewhat shortly. No propitious love affair had ever grown up out of good nature. You may found one on cruelty, on indifference, on bad temper, even on pity, but "good nature" and "good to his mother" will rarely lead to the altar.

"Yes," Elizabeth went on, when she had

donned a fresh shirtwaist, and had come into my room to struggle with its neckpiece. "I did a rather nasty thing to him to-day, and he bore it like a lamb. One of the psychology men told me that they 'd been experimenting with one another, and that Mr. Blight was abnormally subject to suggestion. He acts instantly, and thinks afterward; and to-day, at the literature class, I thought I 'd test him."

I 've often noticed that when Elizabeth wants to be particularly ill-behaved she chooses an occasion when I am not present. I had been obliged to miss literature that morning. It was nice to know that I exercised some moral restraint over my friend, but it gave a heavier significance to John's sense of my responsibility.

"You may go on with your confession," said I; "I shall probably hear all about your latest escapade even if you don't."

"Not a bit of it," she answered, with a mutinous jerk of the head which nearly made her swallow her class pin. "The whole strength of this joke lies in its being known only to Mr. Blight and to me. You know the part of the 'Lady of the Lake,' which Pop Ames had assigned for to-day's recitation."

I nodded acquiescence.

"Well," she went on, "that's more than I did. And more, too, than I think Mr. Blight had mastered. He was sitting just in front of me."

"Madam," I charged her. "Madam, you sneaked into my empty place behind his."

"I told you I was just behind him, and so I could see that he had no more idea of the place than I had, but I kept my ear on Poppy, and when he said: 'We are all familiar [sniffle] with the beautiful passage [sniffle] with which the poem opens, page 220, [rustling of pages all over the room, including mine] with the words:

'The stag at eve had drunk his fill.'

Well, you know Poppy. In five minutes he had a ground plan of that mountain on the blackboard, with all its paths and brooks and ledges and hills, and we were all trailing after the stag barking our shins and getting out of breath, and being treated, in fact, like dogs."

"I know, I know," I comforted her. "He is awful. Do you remember the day he asked why 'Ellen drew her bosom screen'? And how nobody answered, until at last that long, lanky chap from Georgia spoke up and said he 'guessed the mosquitoes must be pretty thick on that lake.' I thought Poppy would burst something, he was so mad."

"Well, you should have seen him to-day. I thought he 'd break everything, especially the first commandment. We had swarmed through underbrush. We were wet and tired, and very hungry; and we were, according to the plan, about ten miles from the scene of the tragedy when the heart-broken huntsman cried:

> 'Woe worth the chase, woe worth the day
> That cost thy life, my gallant Gray.'

Poppy kept his pointer going around in mad circles to show where the dogs were — I 'm

not making a pun — and the other hunts-
men. Suddenly he pounced — you know
his way — upon Billy Blight with: 'And upon
which *side* of the mountain, sir, was the stag
at this time?' Mr. Blight heaved himself
to the perpendicular without a single idea
in his head. He told me afterward that
he'd tramped all over that ground with his
father, and had the whole thing mapped
out for him by one of the gillies. He was
imagining himself back there again. He
knows infinitely more about it than anybody there, including Poppy Ames, and yet
there he stood silent, embarrassed, until
I remembered the psychology man, and
whispered, 'outside.' 'On the outside,'
answered Billy, and sat down triumphant
and calm. But Poppy Ames was not calm.
He hopped up and down and shook his fist,
while the whole class shook with laughter.
And even my belated amendment to Billy,
'south side,' transmitted through a din which
only his voice could pierce did not soothe

our Poppy, and I really should not have cared to be among the boys and girls we met coming in as we were going out. Poppy was still purple, and still jerking his arms and legs, and he was almost swearing at the janitor woman whom he had summoned to wash away his mountain. What I like best about the whole thing is that Billy Blight, when he came to me afterward, said the joke was a 'bird,' distinctly 'on' him, and that he was mine to command for any kind of a luncheon or dinner which you and I would honour him by accepting."

From this time on Billy was safe from Elizabeth, but no one else was safe from either of them. For years we had enjoyed immunity from all the never new yet never palling practical jokes from which other colleges suffered. We were not that kind. We were busy with life and attainment, and comparative Salary and Art Education in Friesland, under the great Mynheer Wimpje Dokkumer; or the Spread of Sloyd in Brussels,

under Hindeloopen Simonzoon. But now
we would be dragged forth from these cool
retreats of learning to find the good old
pranks — with generally a slight topical tinge
— taking possession of our once peaceful
groves. In rather more rapid succession
than would have been normal, had we not
so much time to make up, our Faculty was
called upon to take action upon such lunges
away from our true self as a mild case of
hazing or two — intensely enjoyed by the
victims and only reported through the jealousy
of the unhazed audience. Then there was
the night when a Great Man came to lecture
upon a Great Subject, and somebody put
three ten-grain quinine pills into the cut
glass water pitcher without which no lecturer
is complete.

Let no one suppose that we had ever
ignored the important principle of relaxation.
We knew it to be essential to development,
and so we conscientiously relaxed from time
to time. Occasionally a trolley trip to some

point of interest, historical or artistic, was allowed to break the golden tedium of our days. Less occasionally we had luncheons; but our most frequent dissipation was the reception which made no great demand upon either the exchequer or the wardrobe. Knowing the value of the social spirit, we were always ready to drink chocolate and to eat Huntley & Palmer's wafers upon the invitation of the Library Committee, Trustees, any of the Departments, or any of the classes. Nobody ever seemed to enjoy these affairs with any great intensity; yet only the very strong-minded — and these principally among the Faculty —stayed away from them. Least frequently we broke out into an innocuous revel of dancing, beginning at the bucolic hour of eight, and extinguished by the janitor at half-past ten. He did it with a key and a switchboard, and was most heartless about it.

"Sure, it 's time," he remarked to Elizabeth, who was once deputed to plead for an hour's grace, "for thim poor ould deluthered ladies to be in their beds instid of hoppin' around two be two up there in the studio. The likes of thim 'at school! I'd as soon expect me ould woman to learn anything as one of thim. She's not half the age of some of thim, bedad, and she with six childer."

These festivities always took place in the large studio because it lent itself easily to decoration. The small outside studio, devoted in ordinary times to drawing from cast, served as a coat room. And it was at one of these relaxations that I began to fear that Elizabeth and Billy Blight were in some way concerned in the series of upheavals which had been rending our classic bosom. They were both at the dance — a most unusual thing. An unmarried male was as 'rare as a dodo bird, and the married samples who braved the bedazzlement of our mature charms were dragged there by their wives unmistakably, and danced with by their wives uninterruptedly. Billy and Elizabeth, as I say, were present. They were also glaringly late; but, of course, as they were rarely in time for a lecture, it surprised no one very much that half an hour should be allowed to elapse between Miss Snyder's giggling entrance and the appearance of Miss Alvord and Mr. Blight. It was only afterward that this discrepancy in time came home to me. On that evening I was as much at sea as anyone when the unseen janitor playfully extinguished the lights about five minutes before our allotted time.

Of course we all bolted for the cloak room. The racks were empty, and even in the dark the room seemed full of strange objects. The moonlight from the windows flowed in uninterrupted, though it should have been broken and lost in the line of life-sized classic Greek and Roman casts, which our newest trustee had presented to us. Then the lights flared up again. Then Bedlam, in soprano, broke out. For all our Greek and Roman guests had been lifted to the

floor and dispersed, some singly, some in
groups upon it. The majority of them were
dressed as for the street. At the door stood
Aphrodite, with her head wrapped lightly
in a pink "fascinator." She wore a fur-lined
cloak, and the mystery of her lost arms was
neatly solved by the muff she was resting on
her slightly upraised knee. Beside her stood
Hermes. He looked like pictures of Henry
E. Dixey in "Adonis." He wore a large
silk hat, which I have never seen before nor
since, and a student's cloak, which Billy had
acquired in Paris, and still sometimes wore
in the evening. Aphrodite was looking at
him with her pure, far gaze, and he with out-
stretched arm was offering her a lemon.
Other statues, dressed, or "as is," stood
about among the chairs and tables, and
unless you have seen life-size statues off their
pedestals and down on the floor, you can form
no conception of what that studio was like.
Another Venus, this one with arms, was
crouched against an easel so that only the

curve of her shoulder and her back was visible. In this position she was utterly unrecognizable, and she looked so peculiar that Mrs. Pearson rushed across and threw a shawl about her.

"Land sakes alive!" shrieked Mrs. Morgan, when, feeling a presence at her side, she turned to find herself face to face with a gentleman whose eyes were fixed on a point a thousand miles away, and who seemed crouched to spring at her. "Don't you throw that plate at me, and ain't you ashamed to stand around so?"

Now, if Mrs. Morgan had met that gentleman in any museum from Cork to Cairo, on a pedestal, be it always understood, she would have named him unhesitatingly; and she would have dilated upon him with great purity of expression. Not only the Discobulos has lost distinction by getting off his pedestal.

Mrs. Morgan was hardly silenced when the door opened and the president of the college walked in. He had, he said, on his way across the campus, heard sounds of alarm, and had come to investigate. Now Prexy's eyes were not of the best. And long usage has made him accustomed to shake hands upon the slighetst provocation. He, therefore, cordially grasped Hermes's lemon and found himself during the ensuing quarter of an hour rather puzzled as to how to dispose of it. Then he put on his glasses and surveyed the room carefully. He went mincing about, examining Miss Morton and the Discobolus, Miss Jones and Psyche, Miss Alvord and Aphrodite, with much the same interest and amazement. Finally he encountered Billy.

"Eh! Mr. Blight," said he, "what's the meaning of all this?"

"It looks, sir," he was answered with much deference, "as though the lower class men — or women — are having a joke on us. It's rather a good one, don't you think?"

"Capital! capital!" cried Prexy, tossing his lemon from hand to hand; "but hardly — well, you know — eh?"

"Oh, I don't know!" said Billy grandly. "They don't see the harm and they do see the fun; and I, for one, don't begrudge it to the poor things."

"Of course not, of course not," Prexy agreed, and then, as Elizabeth and I strolled toward them: "Oh! Miss Alvord, and what do you and Miss Blake think of all this?" I have known Elizabeth long enough to be sure that it was the pride of achievement which added such pretty emphasis to her:

"Indeed, I think it's altogether delightful. Several of the students have told me that they never enjoyed anything half so much; and I think you will admit that it seems to be promoting acquaintance and chattiness to a wonderful extent."

"Nevertheless," said I, "if I may be allowed to make a suggestion, I should say that Mr. Blight, who is as strong as he is kind, should stay behind after the others go and restore the statues to their original positions. Then when the lower classes assemble in the morning they will find their greatest effect nullified. They are, of course, looking forward to the consternation and indignation of Professor Blaisdell." I deemed it safer, while making this suggestion, to look straight at Prexy.

"I quite agree with you," he answered. "We must keep the occurrence from Professor Blaisdell. I should especially regret his hearing that I had known of it, and had taken no action. Therefore, I think it would be well for me to retire now," Prexy was not of the stuff that volunteers are made of, "and leave Mr. Blight to his really Herculean efforts." By this time the students had found their wrappings, and as Prexy disappeared in the last bevy of them, I called to him: "And if you should see the janitor, perhaps you will even make a point of seeing him, you might instruct him to come to Mr. Blight's assistance."

"Well, you beat the devil!" said Billy

Blight, looking at me, half malevolent and half amused. "You certainly beat the devil!"

"Yes, does n't she, at putting one and one together?" cried Elizabeth rapturously. And Billy was all malevolent after that betrayal.

VI

ELIZABETH'S AUNT ELIZABETH

A ND now," said Professor Blaisdell, when he had neatly tabulated our names, our ages, our nationalities, and the length of time we had spent at college, "now I must ask you for the name of your parent or guardian; some responsible person with whom I can, from time to time, confer upon your progress."

I looked at Elizabeth and Elizabeth looked at me. Here was Blaisdell breaking out again, and in the worst of possible ways. He had been rather decent since the night at the museum, but he was now going to write home to our people; to send them reports; to keep them stirred up generally. What, then, would become of our boasted independence? Our maiden bachelorhood?

For years we had lived alone in our castle, a law unto ourselves and to one another. Occasionally a visiting relative stayed with us for some space, but we were accustomed, and we had accustomed them, to look upon their comings and goings as entirely dependent upon our pleasure and hospitality; and this idea of Blaisdell's was as new as it was distasteful.

Elizabeth and I were alone with him. He had chosen to interview his victims two by two in his private office, for this little inquisition. And, since our initials were A and B, we were bound to one another by the alphabet as well as by inclination. Elizabeth should have been the first to answer, but she always left disagreeable duties to me, and so I found myself divulging the name and address of my long-suffering mother, wondering, meanwhile, whether the ogre would drag her to New York to listen to the tale of my delinquencies.

Then he turned to Elizabeth. Now, she

has been an orphan since she was three weeks old — that was twenty-one years ago — so she is by this time moderately well accustomed to her bereavement. And if anything could console one for the loss of one's father and mother I think it would be a board of three trustee-uncles like hers — the most indulgent, lovable, and loving old gentlemen who ever wore mutton-chop whiskers and white spats. I had enjoyed a large share of their affection, Elizabeth having sold me a niecehood to them in exchange for a half interest in my mother, and. I was naturally surprised and disconcerted at her reception of the professor's question:

"And your parents, Miss Alvord, where shall I communicate with them?" Elizabeth looked at him and gradually went to pieces. Her upper lip began to quiver and two large tears welled up into her large eyes and hung for a moment on her long, black lashes. She has often tried to teach me this trick, but I never, somehow, can quite get it. I can

produce the tears, but they always flop
unbecomingly out on my cheeks, while Elizabeth, looking every moment sadder and
braver, can swallow hers again. She did this
now, and then turned appealingly to me;
anyone looking at her — even I who know
her so well — might have thought that emotion had robbed her of the power of speech.
The professor's eyes, troubled, embarrassed,
followed hers, and I rebelliously made answer
— she could quite as well have done it herself:

"Miss Alvord's mother and father are both
dead."

"Dear me, dear me, too bad!" said he;
for, though an ogre, he had a heart for such
distress as this. "Are there, perhaps, any
grandparents?" This time Elizabeth found
her voice. She brought those tears back
to the surface, made a great effort, and produced, huskily:

"All dead."

"Then with whom," he asked in the apolo-
getic manner of one who knows that he is

sandpapering a bleeding heart, "with whom may I communicate, as may from time to time become necessary?"

And that ungrateful girl, with her Uncle Charles's latest gift—an amethyst stock-pin —upon her breast, looked pensively down at her hands, twiddled the pearl ring which Uncle John gave her at Christmas round the sapphire ring with which Uncle Peter marked her last birthday, and made reply:

"There is no one, no one at all, who would be interested, except Miss E. H. Alvord, of 527 West 126th Street."

Her own name! And Marthana Caruth's address!

"An aunt?" he suggested.

"Yes," said she.

"Thank you," said he.

"Not at all," said she. And the interview was over.

Very soon, indeed, did Professor Blaisdell find it necessary to communicate to Miss E. H. Alvord the distressing news that her

niece had, upon six consecutive and unexplained occasions, absented herself from his
course in historic art. Marthana Caruth
hopped over to our apartment, all sentimental
interest.   Any one of us who was accustomed
to Elizabeth was also accustomed to sentimental interest, and Marthana had always
an absorbing love for what she called "the
candelstine."   Elizabeth was not in at the
moment, and Marthana vented her excitement upon me. "It's from the college,"
she purred.   "I wonder who it can be from?
I can tell it's a man from the way he makes
his capital 'E.'   But why should anybody
in the college want to write to her?   She's
there every day.   And if he did want to write
to her, why didn't he send the letter here?
How did he know that she knew me so well?
And how——"   Fortunately Elizabeth came
in just then, and we explained the situation to
Marthana and thereby threw her into romantic flutterings and prognostications.

"But why," she demanded at last, when

we had answered all her other questions, "why does he write to Miss Elizabeth H. Alvord? Your name is Elizabeth M., is n't it?"

"Oh, that," said Elizabeth, "is symbolism. You 've read 'Martin Chuzzlewit'?" Marthana nodded vaguely. "And you remember Mrs. Harris? Mrs. Gamp's great friend?" Marthana shook her head this time, but she was still vague. "Then that 's the point," laughed Elizabeth. "My aunt's second name is Harris, because there 'ain't no sich a person.' 'H' is the symbol of Harris. Harris is the symbol of the non-existent. There you have it."

Marthana wrestled in spirit for some moments, and then asked practically and admiringly:

"And what are you going to do next?"

"Oh, next," answered Elizabeth unconcernedly, "you are going to write to Professor Blaisdell." Marthana gasped and protested, but Elizabeth ignored her distress and went serenely on. "I'll tell you what to say, but neither Marion nor I can do the actual writing, because he knows our 'fists.' You will tell him how distressed you are, and how you have laboured and remonstrated with me; how you have even made me a subject of prayer." But here Marthana rebelled.

"I will not pray for you," said Marthana; "that I will not do."

"All right," said Elizabeth leniently, "I will do it for myself. But you *will* copy what I write? Dear Marthana?"

So we three concocted a letter; Elizabeth and I contributed the sentiments, and Marthana set them down in her convent-trained hand.

On the next afternoon I was walking across the campus when I met Professor Blaisdell.

"Do you," he asked amiably, "know Miss Alvord, Senior?" For a moment I hesitated, and so, of course, was lost.

"I do," I answered.

"She must be a very charming woman," he commented; "I judge from a letter which I

So we three concocted a letter

received this morning. I have rarely known anyone who combined such sensibility of mind with such facility of expression. Is Miss Alvord, Senior, advanced in years?"

"Well, of course," said I, "she is older than the younger Miss Alvord."

"She writes with charming grace and culture," he remarked.

"Well," I admitted, "she is very charming."

"So I should have imagined. It is a great privilege for you and your friend to associate with a woman of her type."

I thought, after this, that he showed a new consideration for Elizabeth, and she was so interested in her rôle of aunt that she went quite placidly through the routine of the days; so that Professor Blaisdell felt constrained to report her progress to Miss Alvord, Senior. Elizabeth replied in a masterly epistle in which she expressed, among other things, her satisfaction that her niece had come under the influence of a dominant personality, which was moulding her so wonderfully for the better.

Professor Blaisdell was delighted with himself, and the other students were amazed at the alteration in his treatment of Elizabeth. He no longer frowned upon her levity and suppressed all her remarks. He treated her with a fatherly regard, and she treated him with a yielding sweetness which was one of the most dangerous of her many beguilements. Billy Blight might glower and remonstrate — he did — but this was too serious a misdemeanour for his irresponsible coöperation and he was left unenlightened, gloomy, and unbearable. Only when she and I were alone was she her natural, mischievous, delightful self. At all other times she wore a pensive, chastened air, as though the responsibility of being aunt to a college senior were a thing to be carefully lived up to, and the letter of the series which gave her most pleasure was that in which Blaisdell wrote:

Has it ever, madam, occurred to you that your niece is of a peculiarly impressionable nature and those interested in her welfare should endeavour to surround her with char-

acters whose influence upon her will be for good ?   I question
very much whether Miss Blake exerts such an influence.
Your niece's affection for her friend is very touching and
very beautiful, and, personally, I find Miss Blake entirely
unobjectionable, but in my endeavour to account for the
fluctuations of Miss Alvord's temperament I am forced to
the conclusion that she finds the stimulus for those regrettable lapses from her true self in her association with this
young person.

There is no gratitude in Elizabeth. There
is even no decent feeling; and why I bear
with her, forgive her, cling to her, is more than
I can understand; for there she had a heaven-
sent opportunity of telling Professor Blaisdell
how good I really was and am to her, and
yet her answer to his letter — she showed
me a copy after she had despatched the
original — ran:

I have frequently, and with much concern, suspected that
the influence of Miss Blake over my poor girl is not all that
it should be. Your letter encourages me to think that I
was right, and your kindness.emboldens me to ask for your
advice. I am, I hope, a Christian, God-fearing woman.
Can I therefore, by separating these girls, remove from poor,

dear Marion the one influence for good which is left to her?
Her mother, a devoted and over-indulgent woman, is far from
her child, and to withdraw my Elizabeth — by far the better
balanced of the two — would be to leave Marion to the
guidance of her own erratic tendencies. Do you think I
should be justified in this? Pray let me have your opinion
upon this point.

I let Elizabeth have my opinion, for I
thought, and I still think, that letter an
abominable piece of treachery. She only
laughed in her large and debonair fashion,
and promised that if I would be very good,
her aunt would write and tell Professor
Blaisdell so. It seemed to me that Elizabeth
did not deserve the unbroken success which
attended her in the matter of her aunt. So
upon the next afternoon I arrayed myself
in my best "bib and tucker" and stood
ostentatiously near the bulletin board where
I knew that Professor Blaisdell must pass.

"A beautiful afternoon, Miss Blake," said
he, and went on his preoccupied way. But
I, on vengeance bent, fell into step beside
him.

"Beautiful indeed," I agreed, as we struck across the campus; "and I am going to spend it in such a pleasant way. I am going for a drive with Miss Alvord, Senior. You know her, I think? She speaks so often of you." I had at least succeeded in arresting his attention, and the other girls, studying, and walking, and resting under the trees, must have marvelled to see the earnest interest with which this most *blasé* member of our Faculty spoke to me.

"I have never had the pleasure of actually meeting her, but we frequently exchange letters. How delightfully she writes!"

"Ah, but you should hear her talk," said I, and with a feeling that I was shooting an arrow into the air I added, "you should see her." This last was not as wild a shot as I had expected it to be.

"Does her niece resemble her?" he asked.

"Slightly," I admitted, with a glad return to truth; "perhaps even markedly. Some people think Elizabeth the prettier of the two, but Miss Alvord appeals more to me. Don't you think a woman of thirty-five can still be good looking?"

"Most assuredly I do," he answered — we had looked up the dates of his various diplomas in the *College Announcement* and had decided that he must be forty-two or three — "most decidedly!"

"Well, so do I," said I, "and I know she would be delighted to see you. She is so interested in everything relating to Elizabeth. Why don't you go to see her?"

"I shall," he assured me, as we parted, "I shall make a point of it."

"Do," I encouraged him, "you would be charmed. Everyone loves her." And in his very next letter — it was about Elizabeth's non-attendance at clay modelling — he suggested most formally that an interview would enable him to lay the case before her more fully than he could do in letters. This proposal rather staggered Elizabeth, and for some days she worried about it. Then one morning at breakfast she appeared with a serene brow and told me that her aunt was ill; had been suffering with a severe cold, and was leaving town for Lakewood that afternoon. She read me the letter in which this news was communicated to Professor Blaisdell, and its peroration ran:

The solicitude with which I leave my sweet girl practically alone in this great city is mitigated by the reflection that, in case of necessity, she would have the advantage of your guidance and advice. I cannot say with what pleasure I look forward to making your acquaintance upon my return to town; and I trust my enforced absence will not be of long duration.

By this time Marthana Caruth was in such a state of flutters that she was actually unsafe as a conspirator, and so Elizabeth's aunt ceased for a time to busy herself with Elizabeth's affairs, and the game languished for a while, as other interests overshadowed it. The professor made most polite inquiries and sent most courteous messages. Elizabeth replied to the one and undertook to transmit the other, but there was no tangible evidence of the elder Miss Alvord's existence for two or three weeks, and the younger Miss Alvord, deprived of this support and control, reverted to her earlier, unregenerate state. I could see that the professor attributed this change to me, and I am glad to feel that I had nothing to do with the climax of her wickedness. I was not even at college on the day it occurred. Perhaps if I had been I might have managed to palliate her offence, as many and many a time I had done. I was in bed, very uncomfortably, with tonsilitis, when Elizabeth, refreshed by her long virtue, broke out again.

There is a department of domestic science in our college, and as straw is to bricks, so is milk to domestic science. Therefore, at ten o'clock every day, a high, red-painted, rakish-looking milk-wagon, attached to a tall, rakish-looking chestnut horse, and driven by a red-haired youth of surly temper, rattles up to the gate of learning. The rakish horse is tied, protesting, to the gate-post, while the young man delivers the milk, and not all the months of the scholastic year could accustom Elizabeth to the tableau of that fretting, humiliated steed. She loved horses as she loved nothing else, save mischief, and she always vowed that the milkman's horse had seen better days.

Now, upon the morning that my tonsilitis reached its crisis, Elizabeth and the milkman's horse met — all unchaperoned and unattended — at the college gate. Glances of mutual understanding had frequently passed between them, but never before had they been entirely alone. Now, however, eye held eye for a long, telepathic moment. She smiled. He stretched forth an appealing neck and cocked a knowing eye back at the high, empty seat of the milk-wagon. She looked up at the bright blue sky, at the blind, uncurtained windows of the college, at the leafless trees of the campus and at the empty, sunlit road which led to the open country.

They were still alone.

He pricked his ears toward the empty, sunlit road; *she* glanced up at the high and empty seat.

Presently the milkman, flushed with his daily encounter with the elevator boy, emerged from the high halls of learning and stood aghast. Beside him stood the elevator boy, and they gazed spellbound upon the empty space before them. Yet not quite empty, for upon the curb a neat little heap of text books reposed, and the roadway was punctuated with milk-cans large and small, milk-bottles empty and full, a long-handled dipper, and a book with fluttering yellow leaves. The milkman made a remark the elevator boy echoed, then supplemented it with another still more remarkable.

And out upon the country road, hatless, singing and happy, a tall girl sat in a tall milk-cart, with the name of a well-known dairy upon the red glory of its dashboard, while a tall horse pranced along, head up, crest arched, as he once more felt the touch of a practised driver on the reins and heard no rattle of tin cans behind him.

Many versions of that day's incidents have reached me, but there are two or three facts common to all of them. Everyone agrees that the elevator service was abominable, and since the elevator boy — deaf to bells and heedless to remonstrances — stood upon the steps with his eye upon the road for the two hours which separated Elizabeth's disappearance from her reappearance, this report seems credible. I am also told, with convincing unanimity, that a horde of Italians appeared upon the campus, where no Italian had ever before been seen, and staggered off under the cans, the bottles, the milk, and the enraged imprecations of the milkman, who was left to the consolation of his enemy, with only the yellow-leaved book for company.

At ten o'clock, when the elopement occurred, the campus was, as I have said, deserted, but at a quarter past twelve, when the fugitives returned, it was swarming with students and

with Faculty surging or trickling out into the
sunshine from the different buildings.   And
upon the steps of Ardmore Hall stood Prexy,
the unapproachable, the austere Prexy, listening restively to the lamentations of the milkman, who had spent the intervening hours
in fruitless telephoning and fruitless recon-
noitering.   You are to picture to yourself the
old gray buildings standing solemnly about the
campus, dignified, austere; the book-laden
students in their caps and gowns, the basket-
ball teams snatching a quarter-hour practice,
the cake-woman in her bright red shawl, the
lemonade man in his white cap, the whole
busy, orderly scene of midday on a college
campus.   And to this scene you are to add
the sudden apparition of a red and brilliant
milk-cart, driven by a girl with wind-tossed
hair and laughing eyes, for Elizabeth, "playing hookey" at twenty-two, was radiantly
unashamed of herself, and sprang to the
ground before the gladdened eyes of the
milkman, with all the air of having done

something extremely creditable. She must have made up her mind to the probable cost of her adventure, for she paid its first instalment with the prettiest air imaginable.

"Ah, dear Mr. Farms — the name is Farms, is it not? Meadowbrook Farms, I see by the dashboard — I have had a most delightful drive, and I hope that this" — and she presented him with a ten-dollar bill and a bewitching smile — "will reimburse you for your expense and anxiety."

But if she were debonair and gay the partner of her flight was not. His guilty head drooped between his feet and every line showed him conscience-stricken and afraid. Yet, even deducting the price of the milk-cans and the scattered milk, he had done a tolerably good morning's work for his master.

Prexy still glowered upon the steps; the basket-ball teams stopped to watch developments; the lunch-bound students halted in the gravel walks; a hush fell over the campus as Miss Alvord mounted the steps, held out her strong little hand in its turned-back dog-skin glove, and exclaimed:

"Ah, Doctor Arnott, it is such an age since I saw you, and I am so sorry that you were not with me this morning! I had a most heavenly drive." And Prexy took the little hand in his, thereby destroying for all time his reputation for austerity, and answered:

"My dear young lady, you are very kind. I should have been delighted."

Now it was all very well for Prexy to be noble and nice about it, but Elizabeth was not in his particular care as she was in Professor Blaisdell's, and that conscientious educator did not propose supinely to allow his students to become horse thieves. Elizabeth confesses that she had a remarkably bad quarter of an hour that afternoon. She flattered herself that she had played her part of the penitent and regenerated sinner with compelling force, but a morning or two later she was undeceived. Marthana Caruth brought us a letter for Elizabeth's aunt;

it was branded "important," and marked "please forward," and it ran:

"My Dear Miss Alvord: Since your departure from New York the regeneration which had manifested itself in your niece's conduct has suffered an unaccountable check. A most regrettable incident took place a few days ago, and, although the president of the college sees fit to overlook it, I cannot feel justified in leniency. Had Miss Alvord been a pupil of the grammar school her offence would be sufficiently reprehensible. In a college senior it is quite inexcusable. I wish it were possible to write you the details, but after several efforts I am forced to abandon the attempt. It is impossible to describe the events without making the account seem either ridiculous or amusing, and I can assure you that it was neither. I trust that you have by now sufficiently recovered to make it possible for you to receive visitors. The events of the past few days have been so disagreeable and perplexing that I feel in need of rest, and have decided to go to Lakewood for the Friday, Saturday, and Sunday of this week. May I look forward to the pleasure of making your acquaintance and discussing some means to the future guidance of your niece upon that occasion?"

Elizabeth read this letter in silence, and in silence she handed it to me. She looked very grave. Presently she asked:

"How has my dear aunt been lately? Do you remember? You 've done most of the reporting."

"She has not been very well," I answered. "Professor Blaisdell has asked for news of her almost every morning, and I have told him that, while there was no immediate danger, we were yet very anxious about her."

"So we are," Elizabeth acquiesced warmly, "worried to death about the poor old dear. What does he mean by writing an exciting letter like that to a poor, sick lady, at Lakewood for her health? Why," she cried in sudden inspiration, "it 's enough to kill her!" And then she broke off to chuckle delightedly:

"Oh, what would I give, what would I *not* give, to see Professor Blaisdell's version of my offence: 'Dear Madam, I grieve to state that your niece stole a milk-wagon.' Or: 'My dear Miss Alvord, whatever shall I do? That bad girl has been and run off with a horse. Shall I punish her, or will you?'

Elizabeth read this letter in silence

Oh Lor', oh Lor'! I wish I could get at his waste-paper basket."

"That 's all very well," said I, "but I should like to ask what you 're going to do next. You can't keep putting him off forever. You know how determined and persevering a man he is, and sooner or later he will call upon your Aunt Elizabeth."

"I think not," she made reply. "I have a premonition" — and she began to call tears into her eyes and a quaver into her voice — "something tells me that she will never live to meet him. She is very near the end. If he asks either of us to-day about her, remember that she has changed alarmingly for the worse, and that she insists upon returning to town; says it 's her sacred duty — no one knows why."

For several days — ever since Elizabeth's drive, to be exact — Professor Blaisdell had confined his inquiries to me, as he considered it beneath his dignity to have anything to do with her. So I máde my report as unfavourable as it well could be, and he was greatly concerned. On the next morning the invalid had returned to town; on the next she was so ill that Elizabeth could not leave her bedside; on the next she was unconscious; and on Friday she was dead, and I stayed at college only long enough to tell him. He was quite overcome, and it was only the realization that this regret would be easier for him to bear than the knowledge that he had been befooled and laughed at that kept me from telling him the truth. The funeral occurred on Monday morning, the busiest time in the week for him, but he sent some exquisite flowers, so beautiful and white that they made us seriously remorseful and ashamed of ourselves until we took them to the hospital and left them in the children's ward. Of course Elizabeth had to stay at home for a week, but she beguiled the hours by evolving the most bewitching mourning I ever saw. She was always pretty, and often beautiful, but in these lovely, soft, black gowns, with dainty white collars and cuffs, she was absolutely lovely. She had a good deal of leisure time on her hands, and in it she evolved, too, the climax of her little comedy.

"My dear friend," it began, "I wish that I might have met you face to face and carried the picture of you with me. But it was not to be. May I hope that, for as long as my dear child remains within the sphere of your influence, you will continue your kind interest in her; that you will be patient and forbearing with her wilfulness, making allowances in your strength for her weakness? I can write no more. Farewell."

I absolutely refused to have anything to do with this effusion, and Elizabeth was obliged to enclose it with a letter in her own hand, telling him that she had found it, sealed, among the papers of her dear aunt. And that very evening he called upon us, and when Margaret handed us his cards on her little silver tray I saw something which nobody else has ever seen: Elizabeth Alvord in a panic of fright. He followed his card so promptly that he was in the room before she could escape, and he was himself so genuinely distressed and so naturally sorry that it was difficult to realize him as the Professor Blaisdell of the lecture room. Of course he accepted Elizabeth's emotion as natural under the circumstances, and he took her hand in both of his in the most kindly, unaffected way; he led her to the divan, tucked a cushion behind her, and examined her face in a professional and almost proprietary manner. She had by this time recovered sufficiently to be tearful again, and I, being utterly and evidently superfluous, and being besides extremely angry with Elizabeth for the length to which she was carrying her game, invented some excuse for leaving the room, and returned to it only when I heard the door close and knew that she was alone. To my amazement I found her, face downward, among the pillows, sobbing as though her heart would break.

"You can stop now," said I crossly; "he's gone, and I hope you are ashamed of yourself."

She cried on.

I found her, face downward, among the pillows, sobbing as though her heart would break

"*I'm* ashamed of you."

Still she wept.

"And I repeat that you are wasting your crocodile tears. There is no one here to be affected by them."

She continued to sob, and presently I discovered her emotion to be genuine. Now, she is peculiar in many ways, but in her weeping she is absolutely original. She does it seldom, but thoroughly, and she never tries to combine speech and sobs. When I had petted her back to calmness and set her upright among the cushions, she spoke:

"He made me cry."

"You richly deserve that he should. What did he say?"

"Everything that was kind. That he considers me a sacred trust from the dead. Me!" And she was so tragic that I thought she intended me to laugh. So I did. Which irritated instead of soothing her.

"He says," she went on, "that he intends to advise me, cheer and comfort me; to help me to correct my recklessness and wilfulness, and to become in every way the sweet and gentle woman which nature — and Aunt Elizabeth — intended me to be."

"Anything else?"

"Nothing else."

"Then why were you crying?"

"Because," she answered, and her pretty eyes were full of real tears and real distress, "because, Marion dear, I have a feeling that he will keep his word."

VII

CRUMBS OF CULTURE

H AVE you," said Billy Blight, "either of you — got 'European Morals'?" Elizabeth and I looked up at him simultaneously, and in doing so we naturally looked at one another, since she was writing at a combination of desk and table in our little drawing room, and I had spread my things on the dining table. There was nothing between these two rooms but an arch partly filled with fretwork arabesque, and in this arch stood the tall gray figure of Billy Blight and the checked gingham outlines of Margaret.

"He would come in, miss, say what I would," she apologized, with one stern and one admiring eye on Billy. "I told him as how the young ladies was particular engaged, but in he comes and says he only wants to ask a question."

"Then ask it," commanded Elizabeth. "We're busy. Have only until to-morrow to finish this comparative philosophy thing. Ask it, and trot!"

"I have asked it," he broke out. "*Have* you 'European Morals,' or have you not?"

"Well, to be sure, sir," cried Margaret. "Don't speak to him, Miss Elizabeth dear, I'll take him to the kitchen. Come, Mr. Billy, there's a good young gentleman. Come with Margaret. A nice black cup of coffee ——" But Billy shook her off.

"Have you got 'em?" he demanded, for the third time.

"Don't know," answered Elizabeth. "What part of Europe, for instance?"

"The whole little shop, I believe. It's a book, as you jolly well know, by a chap called Lecky. One of the references for this very identical paper you're writing, and which I ought to be writing too. I badgered them so about it at the library that at last they told me you had it, and I came around to borrow it."

"I'm sorry, Billy," said Elizabeth, "but I've lent it to Miss Peterson. You know that graduate student whose place is two seats beyond yours at Education I. She lives some place about here. I'll look her up in the Register. Maybe she will let you have it."

"But I never saw her." Billy protested. "I can't walk up to a strange young lady and inquire about morals."

"Nonsense," I interrupted. "You've seen her three times a week when you didn't 'cut.' She's a quiet little thing in spectacles. Now go before you're slain."

Breakfast time the next morning brought Billy back to us. We were then more at leisure to listen to his transports; and he was generally well worth listening to. The son of a famous father, and the grandson of of a famous old martinet, who vowed that she would cut him off with a shilling unless he adopted a profession. So here he was, in our college, preparing to fill the chair of art in some great and still mythical university. "Though they 'd be rum dodgers," he always added, ruefully, "if they 'd give the job to me." No one, not even the dragon Margaret, could resist him; and even Blaisdell, that Nero, accepted, with what grace he might, the boy's superior talent. And it cannot be pleasant for a professor to know that he is far outclassed by one of his students, and to know that the student knows it. But this was only in the actual painting or drawing. In all other subjects treated of in our halls of learning Billy was, as he pathetically described it, a hopeless duffer.

On the morning that he dropped in all uninvited, to breakfast with us, he was so radiantly delighted with himself that Elizabeth and I greeted him in chorus with:

"So you 've finished the paper after all!"

"I forgot it," said Billy, as nearly crestfallen as he knew how to be. "I give you my word, I never thought of it since I was here yesterday afternoon. I found those morals, though," he cheered up to tell us, "and I found Miss Peterson, too. Why did n't you ever tell me," and he turned reproachfully to Elizabeth, "that she has perfectly beautiful eyes? As blue and sweet and innocent as a child's. She 's going to let me do them."

"Ah! Billy, Billy," said I. "You 've been doing it already, and you promised, you know how faithfully you promised, to devote yourself exclusively to your work."

"That 's just what I was doing," he replied with triumph. "I call upon ye both to witness that I went forth in search of 'European Morals,' so that I might finish my paper on philosophy. I 've forgotten every word of it now, but as I was thinking it out it seemed to mean to be a corker. I won't stop to ask you young ladies what morals, even Lecky's morals, have to do with phil- osophy. We 'll let them have that question for some night at the Debating Society. To resume: I went to the address you gave me, and consumed a whole box of matches in reading the names on the bell plates. It 's a flat house, you know. Not a lordly apartment like this in which ye female sybarites loll away your days with an elevator and Margaret. But a regular common or garden variety flat house, where you press the button and you never can tell who does the rest. And there I found Ferguson's name. You know Ferguson, that chap with whiskers, who is nearly always late for Education I when I 'm there."

"He 's generally late when you 're not there too," I supplemented. "He 's always dashing about in a breathless hurry."

"This is my story and my stage," remonstrated Billy. "Again I shall resume. And under Ferguson's name Miss Peterson's was written. 'European, by Jove!' thinks I, when I sees that combination, 'and Southern European, at that.'"

"Now, Billy," said I, threateningly, "you 'll get no more breakfast unless you behave."

"I 'm resuming, I 'm resuming," he pleaded. "I pressed that there bell, the door clicked open, and I walked up past beefsteak and onions on the first floor; past corn beef and cabbage on the second; past Irish stew and coffee on the third — and all in the dark, mind you — past fried ham and eggs on the fourth floor; up to a lady and a baby on the fifth. I could hardly see her face, but I could see the kid's white dress. 'I 'd like to see Miss Peterson,' says I.

"'I am Miss Peterson,' says she. 'Won't you come in?'

"So I followed her into a dark little narrow hall. I give you my word I touched it on both sides, and top and bottom. Then I broke into a room where a dull patch of evening showed through a window. I was just preparing to roar for help. I felt so far from my mother, you know, and everybody I ever loved. And it was ghostly to be in that strange room and not to be able to see anything moving except that white kid sailing through mid-air under the arm of Miss Peterson's dark dress. She seemed to be looking for something, feeling about on table and mantelpiece. 'I can't find the matches,' she said, at last; 'may I trouble you to hold Morgan while I go through to the kitchen?'"

"Oh, Billy!" bubbled Elizabeth; "I'd have given anything to see it."

"The point is that no one could see it," he retorted. "'T was all in the ghostly dark, and there I stood holding that kid, afraid that if I moved it would get upside down or something; while the woman went away and away clear out of hearing."

"A mad woman in my opinion," boomed Margaret from the kitchen door. "Anyone ought to be able to see even in the dark that Mr. Blight is not one to be trusted with babies."

"There she goes," he expostulated, "discrediting me, and interrupting me when I 'm trying to bring a little romance into your empty lives. And I *was* fit to be trusted with babies, though you don't believe it, Margaret. I held that kid up against my shoulder and it gurgled like water under a birch-bark canoe. Then, presently, Miss Peterson came back with the matches, lit the gas, and shook hands with me. I was jolly glad, Miss Blake, that you told me I knew her, for I give you my word I never remember having seen her before. However, she seemed to recognize me" — Billy Blight's six feet of handsome boyhood was not likely to go unobserved. "I began asking her about the 'Morals,' and she said Mr. Ferguson had 'em, and would be in at any moment. And all this time I sat there holding Morgan, and looking him over generally. He 's one of the finest children ——"

"And you know so much about 'em, sir," scoffed Margaret.

"I shall from now on," Billy announced.

"I tell you my friend Morgan is a great little chap. A back as flat as a pancake, and dandy bumps on his head. He let me feel 'em, and never said a word."

"How old is he?" asked Elizabeth.

"Six months, Miss Peterson told me."

"Then that explains his not saying much."

"You do not deserve it. Your conduct is most disagreeable," cried Billy, "and yet I *will* resume. Ferguson came in after a while, and I asked him about the 'Morals.' He never turned a hair, but stalked out of the room and was back again in a minute with the darned old book, and Mrs. Ferguson, who had just come home from a psychology lecture which Ferguson wanted notes on, but had not time to go to. Now there's a wife for you," cried Billy, with a beautiful enthusiasm. "It seems that Ferguson got some sort of scholarship, not half enough, of course, to live on, but he saved some and borrowed some out in the Western town where he was principal of the high school. Then he came East with the missus and the kid, and if he can pull off his Ph. D. this year he can get a better salary and a better position when he goes back. But he told me it's pretty close sailing."

"And Miss Peterson is ballast, I suppose," Elizabeth suggested.

"Yes, she takes a room from them. Lord, a fellow must be badly off for a few letters after his name when he works as Ferguson does for them."

Elizabeth and I, but more particularly I, had much sad knowledge of the straits and makeshifts to which many of the students were reduced. They never seemed able to form any prevision of the enormous expense of life, bare life, in New York. And they were continually giving up, as Mr. Ferguson had, the chicken in the hand for the turkey in the bush. My engagement to John made it natural that I should hear more of the personal life of the student body than the ordinary senior would. The Students' Aid Society, some of the more humanitarian trustees, and even "Prexy" himself, had often allowed me to bridge the abyss which separates noble poverty from the aloofness imposed upon the authorities.

Miss Peterson was herself a case in point. She had taught in country schools in northern New York for more years than Billy Blight would have believed. She had been boarded about in the houses of the better farming class. She had worked long and faithfully, and she had sent all her little savings to an invalid mother in Utica. Four years ago this mother had died, and the daughter had then commenced to hoard all that she might toward the fulfilment of her one supreme ambition — a year of study in the city. She had never missed a lecture. She never wasted a moment. She read far into the night, and long before daylight in the morning; and she learned, inexorably and unanswerably, that it would take not one year, but eight or ten to reach the pinnacle of culture and efficiency at which she aimed.

I was, perhaps, the most intimate friend she had, not only at college, but — as I discovered with an unaccountable sinking of the heart — in the world. The farm people among whom she had passed her life had never satisfied her. They resented as affectations the quaint and self-taught refinements which seemed so pitiful and so provincial to us of broader, happier lives. She told me once, wonderingly, about Billy's first visit. How she was sitting in the dark, realizing all her failures. Little Morgan was asleep in her arms, and as she felt his gentle breathing against her breast she found another pathway to misery. All her thought and effort had been given to children: other women's children; always other women's children. She had written her love upon the shifting sands, and now when she stopped and turned back to read what she had written, the sands were scattered — the writing gone. She held Morgan's warm little body close to her empty heart and prayed for courage, for strength.

Then enter Billy Blight, gay and young, handsome and debonair. You are to remember that, save Ferguson, she had never known what is commonly called a gentleman. And here was one who shone unquestioned, undimmed, even when set among the men of learning and distinction among whom he moved by virtue of his father's name and his own surpassing charm.

"And there he sat, Miss Blake," she told me, "holding Morgan on his knee, and talking the sort of foolishness that sounds like sense, or of sense that sounds like foolishness. He talked "— and her eyes glowed behind their glasses — "as people do in great books. And when he told me how glad he was to meet me, and how often he had watched me sitting just two places from him at Education I, I *was* surprised.

Somehow I did n't think the gentlemen students noticed us young ladies very much."

Oh! Billy, Billy!

From the evening of that first meeting life somehow changed for Miss Peterson. It had been contracted enough before; but now it narrowed down until it meant nothing but Education I, three hours a week! That was the only course of lectures which both Billy and she attended. But the joy, the radiant, shy joy which his mere presence in the room gave her would have served to illuminate a much fuller life. Happiness glowed in her eyes, through her whole face, when he was near, so that she shone resplendent — translated — although she never wore anything but the plain, rather well-made dark blue and green plaid gown which was, somehow, characteristic of her. Also it might mean millions or nickels to the casual eye.

We were quite accustomed to Billy's raptures about his long succession of charmers.

Their number and variety, and his earnestness about them, made his table talk unique.
Their ages ranged from six to sixty — but
the greatest number were at the ends. John
often said that a true record, a regular scientific one, I mean, of Billy's mind would be
a valuable addition to "man's study of man-
kind." So friendly, so crystal clear, so self-
centred, and so generous. He could weep,
openly and unashamed, over the loves and
sorrows in the fifteenth century "chansons"
to which he was devoted; and he could pass
quite unaware through the love and the
sorrow all about him.

Billy Blight was never one to take a new
interest calmly, and we were soon deluged
with reports on Morgan, whose psychology,
down to its last motor reaction, had been
studied and tabulated by Mr. Ferguson
and set forth in a thesis which John reported
to be really admirable. Billy had borrowed
a copy of this thesis and he insisted upon
regarding its observations and conclusions

as so many proofs of Morgan's precocity.
In vain we pointed out to him that the whole
value of the treatise depended upon its being
a study of The Normal Child.

"Normal," he scoffed; "there never was
anything like him. Think of it, when he
was three days old, he closed his fist and
jabbed it in his eye. Here it is. Read it
for yourselves. Did either of you ever see
a three-day-old baby do anything like that?"

"I did not," Elizabeth admitted; "for I
never saw a three-day-old baby. Did you?"

"Oh! Suffering Moses!" groaned Billy.
"There are some persons a fellow simply
can't talk to. They may be decent enough
looking, and all that sort of thing, but they
will ask the most beastly questions. I shall
never again demean my friend Morgan by
mentioning him to you."

Although Billy kept tolerably close to this
last threat of his, we gathered that his intimacy
with the Ferguson ménage continued. He
frequently entertained them — his friend

Morgan always included — in his very luxurious quarters. These domestic festivities must have been in striking contrast to some of those over which he presided, and it was at one of them that he made a remark for which I think he will never quite forgive himself. He told me about it weeks afterward.

"But how was I to know," he cried; "how could anyone have known? Nobody could have known or guessed it, could they Miss Blake?"

"No, no," I soothed him, "Billy dear. Of course, you could n't have known." And yet all the time, from the very beginning, I had marvelled that he could have escaped knowing. It was on a night when he was host to the Fergusons. The occasion was one of Morgan's monthly birthdays, and everything was very gay and very perfect as Billy and his Japanese "boy" knew how to make them. There was ice cream, and with it some sticky, heavy, yet delicious little cakes, the like of which neither the Fergusons nor Miss Peterson had ever tasted.

"I never ate anything so *exquisite*; but I should n't think they 'd be very wholesome," said Miss Peterson. "I suppose you don't eat very many of them."

"I 'd eat a hundred, and think nothing of it," he answered, inconsequent as usual; and, as usual, far overleaping his guest's faint praise. "There 's nothing I would n't do to get them except to *get* them. I 'd beg, borrow, or steal. I 'd go to tea with impossible old ladies, or to lunch with more impossible ones if they 'd lure me with Mailliard's *Petit Fours*."

"You do seem real partial to them," smiled Miss Peterson.

On the next day Elizabeth had, as we afterward realized, an opportunity to avert the not yet inevitable. Perhaps thinking my friend more frivolous than she thought me, Miss Peterson asked her where Mailliard's *Petit Fours* might be obtained. And Elizabeth,

without thought and without inquiry, gave
the desired information and promptly forgot
all about it.   Billy had forgotten too; but
Miss Peterson, grudging car fare, walked
three miles down town (you will say she was
a country girl) and three miles back, and
paid seventy-five cents for one pound of the
sticky, sweet little cakes. Billy had never
expressed a desire to her before. His part
had been all giving: flowers, theatre tickets,
books, and his companionship. To him these
were civilities not quite impersonal, perhaps, for he was above all things kind, and
this forty-year-old child—she was in many
ways no more than child—held him and fas-
cinated him. But such gifts, such atten-
tions as he had shown her were an old story
to him. And they were a part of the lan-
guage of everyday courtesy. The people
among whom he lived so understood, so
accepted them. But here was a creature,
a woman, to whom the last petal of his last
flower was a treasure — who held the very

boxes precious. Nothing was a matter of course to her. Her god was forever popping in and out of his machine like a jack-in-the-box, and showering favours as he moved. She never knew or dreamed that he was being ordinarily and quite conventionally polite. And she had such a genius for communicating her pleasure that Billy felt every throb of the joy he gave, and spent his kindly heart in devising ever new ways of giving and sharing happiness.

"Take her to the theatre," he told us once, "and, before the curtain goes up on the second act, she 'll make you feel that the play is a masterpiece; that you wrote it; and that you could beat the leading man to a standstill if you had n't something more important to do. And take her to the Opera ——"

"Have you ?" I asked.

"Two or three times. You never saw anything like her enjoyment. It 's dreadful to think of her being shut away from it

all for so many years. She told me quite
frankly that she had expected to 'do' the
musical season rather thoroughly, but that
the prices staggered her. She was so concerned at my buying tickets that I had to
tell her my father gave them to me. Then
she settled down to 'absorb,' and I tell you
she did n't miss much. She even reads the
'libretto,'" he marvelled. "One never thinks
of that, you know." 'T was little he knew
of the eager soul in search of culture.

I think it is not necessary to say that she
loved him. Emotion had hardly touched her
before, and now it racked her. But she
hid it with all the shy, sweet reserve which
belongs to love's youngest dreams. I think
that only I guessed the secret, and I never
should have done so if it were not for loving
John. Billy never had the faintest suspicion. He went to tea with her almost
daily now, and she made almost daily trips
to Mailliard's. 'T was the one way in which
she could pleasure him, and he was always

pleasuring her. Somehow it touched the mother in her heart that his desire should be so boyish. Little cakes! Sweet, soft, sticky little cakes! After the third or fourth of her expeditions downtown she stopped to see the woman who, for three dollars a week, supplied her with what they agreed to call three meals a day.

"If you don't mind," she faltered, "I'll settle with you now. I'm thinking of getting board where I have my room. It would be more convenient, you see."

"I'll be sorry to lose you," the woman answered, "and the other young ladies at your table will feel the same, I'm sure. You was real friendly together. But, of course, you must suit your own convenience."

"It's not so much that," said Miss Peterson; "thank you for your kindness to me — and — good-bye."

Neither then nor at any subsequent time did she broach the matter of board to Mrs. Ferguson. She made no other arrangements,

and she had no facilities to prepare anything, but tea, in her own room. It was,
as we afterward computed, about three
weeks after this that Billy decided to spend
a day at home with a pipe and a novel.

There was no transfiguring joy in Miss
Peterson's face that day to disguise its woe-
ful emaciation. She was evidently hurt and
surprised by something which had already
occurred, and Billy's failure to turn up at
Education I seemed almost to paralyze her.
She sat in her place watching the door, half
blindly, for some chance remark of his had
caused her to discard her spectacles, until
it was plain that he would not be there.
She seemed almost unconscious of the rest
of us, and several times during the ensuing
hours I saw the tears spring from under her
closed lids. Naturally, I waylaid her in the
hall; but she seemed timid and ill, and most
keenly anxious to get away from me; and it
was really in a sort of desperation that I
asked her whether she had seen Billy lately.

I simply could not see a creature suffer so without trying to find the cause and the cure.

"Not since Monday." It was then Thursday. "I 've been a little lonely lately," she amplified sadly; "Mr. and Mrs. Ferguson were called back home to attend her father's funeral. They left Monday night, and they took Morgan. But I 'm expecting Mr. Blight this afternoon. He often drops in to tea, and if you 'll excuse me I 'll go right along now and see that it 's all ready for him." She swayed a little as she spoke, and her face seemed to be all eyes: Eyes blue, and sweet, and innocent as a child's, Billy had called them; and even the pain and fright that filled them now were childlike, surprised. She wanted, I foolishly decided, just one thing; and she should have him to tea that afternoon if I had to drag him there.

I telephoned to his apartment, and learned that he 'd gone down to see some new work of his father's. I telephoned to Mr. Blight's studio, and was told that the father and son had gone out together.

"Do you think," I asked, "that you could find them ?"

"I 'll try, madam," the man answered. "I 'll call up one or two of the clubs."

"And if you find them," I charged him, "tell Mr. Blight, Junior, that a friend of his is ill, and that Miss Blake wants to see him immediately."

It was quite two and a half hours later — which made it about seven o'clock — when Margaret ushered him in. I had told Elizabeth as much as was necessary of what I guessed, or knew, or feared, and she left me alone with Billy after the merest of greetings.

"Who is it ?" he demanded instantly.

"Miss Peterson," said I. "When have you seen her ?"

"On Monday."

"And since then you 've dropped her ?"

"And a jolly cad I 'd have been if I had n't stopped going there. Don't you know the

Fergusons are away?   Don't you know that that's the reason I've not been there?   How could I have gone?   What would you have thought of me if I had?"

"You should have explained it to her. She does n't understand much about convention, and she's hurt.   We'll go together now," said I, as I adjusted my hat before the mirror, and threw my jacket at him.   "She's never had an inkling of your reason, and she's been expecting you since half-past four o'clock this afternoon."

Except that we were met by no welcome after our five stairs' climb our experiences and sentiments closely reproduced Billy's first impressions.

"She's in," he said, as the door yielded to his hand.   "They only lock up when they're going out."

I entered the dark little hall.   I stood in the drawing room while Billy found a match, and lit the flaring gas.   And very patiently and quietly Miss Peterson was waiting in a chair beside the tea table on which the tea pot had long grown cold. There were two cups upon the table, and a plate high heaped with sticky, heavy little cakes. Everything was very still. Only the gas shrieked and laughed above us as Billy turned to his hostess. Well, we were in time. By some miracle we were just in time. Billy, by another miracle, produced a cab, and in a few minutes Elizabeth and Margaret were in a whirl of hospitality and blankets.

It was purely, the doctor assured us, a case of exhaustion from lack of nourishment, and when Margaret heard this pronouncement you can imagine her joy and activity. Nothing in the whole course of our college life gave her a keener delight than the nursing of Miss Peterson, but during the first few days shadows passed across her pleasure. Her patient was occasionally quietly delirious, and on these occasions Margaret, with a kindly, puckered brow, would summon Elizabeth — always Elizabeth — to the bedside,

And Elizabeth, rejoining me when speech had passed, and sleep had come, seemed serious, puzzled, perhaps a little wistful. She grew very gentle during that week, and her manner to Billy Blight lost some of its flippant disregard.

Presently Miss Peterson grew quite herself again, and John secured her a position in the library. She still sees Billy as often as ever; does wonderful shifting of the order cards when he condescends to want a book, and understands as clearly as I what Billy feels for Elizabeth and what Elizabeth feels for Billy. And, living daily in expectation of his becoming the great man of the age, she manages to make herself content.

VIII

MADE IN HEAVEN

NO HEATHEN of the wilds could have resisted conversion more persistently and with more spirit than Elizabeth displayed when Professor Blaisdell saw it in the light of his duty to the dead to turn her from her ways of frivolity and cheer into the narrow path of the perfect student. All the college saw and wondered at his perseverance. All the college saw and sympathized with his frequent disappointments, but gradually and surely he made his effect, and gradually and slowly Elizabeth yielded to his influence, and we who loved her in her native high-spirited mischievous state could do nothing.

Our flat grew to be a cheerless spot and Margaret fell into a dreary routine of French chops and scrambled eggs. Without the

inspiration of Elizabeth's nonsense and gay
badinage she could not manage even a cake
or a *soufflè* for us. Like poor Mr. William
in the Bab Ballads: "Our spirits, once so
buoyant, grew uncomfortably low."

Even the general atmosphere of the lecture
rooms and studios felt the change, and the male
student body lounged lifeless in the background and glared, as Blaisdell suppressed,
kindly and leniently but with deadly certainty,
every one of Elizabeth's little flares of gaiety.
Things went with a horrible regularity. Blaisdell glowed — or rather he was gently suffused
— with satisfaction and high purpose. We
drew, we painted, we learned history of art,
of education, of the United States, or the pre-
Raphaelite movement with the same unbroken
calm. Visitors came and marvelled at us.
Other professors heard and wondered how long
the thing would last.

John and I agreed perfectly upon every
subject, save this one. He had long known
and admired Blaisdell, and he considered him

a most desirable *parti* for Elizabeth.   Now I had long known and admired Elizabeth, and I did n't consider Blaisdell one-tenth good enough for her.   She was gay and young and clever;   he was serious, middle-aged, and learned.   At his first coming to college I had for a time hoped that, by adaptations and concessions on both sides, John's idea might work out, and it would have been heavenly for me to have Elizabeth also a Faculty wife.   I always rather dreaded that part of my future life which was to be spent among the wives of John's colleagues.

But when Blaisdell had made himself responsible for Elizabeth's mental and moral uplift, and she had tamely submitted to being uplifted, I began to see that she never could be happy with him; that all the adaptation and all the concession would be done by her, and that she would change — as she was already beginning to show signs of changing — into an insufferable prig.

It was as much fear of him as anything

else which changed her, and she had ample cause for fear. We lived, she, Marthana and I, in the tangled web of which Dr. Watts speaks. After we had killed Miss Alvord, Senior, and considered the incident closed, it was really only just beginning. For Professor Blaisdell persisted in carrying out his dear friend's last wishes and upon seeing a great deal of his sacred charge. We all lived in daily horror of his coming in contact with one of her uncles or with some friend who would enlighten him.

I now think that she never had the slightest idea of marrying him, and she insists that he never had the slightest idea of marrying her; but he certainly was attentive to her and developed a habit of calling upon her an evening or two every week, and though they never discussed anything more personal or interesting than his lectures, past or future, they yet saw a great deal of each other, and gave palpable grounds for John's hope and Margaret's fear. Margaret was all for the young Lochinvar type of suitor. Even John, though she liked him, she considered a little staid and settled for the rôle, but for Blaisdell's supposed pretensions she felt nothing but scorn and fear.

I was reading up some history of art references in the little drawing room of our little flat one February afternoon. The late silence was broken only by the sound of Margaret's heavy footfall and heavier dirge. She was preparing our French-chop, boiled-potato, green-peas dinner, and as she vacillated between dining room and kitchen she demanded, in a horrid minor croon, "Where is my wandering boy to-night?"

Suddenly Elizabeth's key clicked in the door and presently she was perched on the arm of my Morris chair.

"I'm going to marry Professor Blaisdell," she announced.

"You are not!" said I. "Never, so long as I have strength to forbid the banns. I shall tell him that your Aunt Elizabeth appeared to me in a vision and objected to it."

At this she fell away in helpless laughter, the most really Elizabethan laughter I had heard for many and many a day. Margaret paddled in from the kitchen in a wreath of smiles, and I rose up out of my Morris chair and cast myself upon my friend.

"I 'm not going to marry him," she managed at last to assure me, "in the way you mean, at least. Such a thought never entered his well-informed and logical head. I mean that I shall choose a suitable bride for him. And soon. For if the idea of marrying me ever *should* occur to him, I don't know what would happen. He has a way of expecting me to do just as he thinks best. And all because of his admiration for my Aunt Elizabeth."

When the full scope of Elizabeth's plan of escape filtered into my "fringe of consciousness," as the psychology man used to say, I saw at once its manifold perfections and its one insuperable difficulty.

"*Cherchez la femme,*" said I.

"I'll get her," cried Elizabeth, with a palpable flash of her old spirit. "I'll get her if I have to invent her. Did n't I invent an aunt? A bride is no more difficult. And did n't he fall in love with the aunt? He did n't, of course, recognize the symptoms, but some of his later letters troubled themselves not overmuch about me. If she had lived — lived ——"

"I'm beginning to think," I interrupted, "that you believe in her."

"You'll all believe in the bride," she promised. "How old should you advise me to have her?" and she spent the next half hour in choosing the attributes most suitable to a helpmate for Blaisdell. None of them sparkled very ostentatiously in her own diadem, but I noticed that she treated him most generously. She seemed to have a sincere liking for him and a keen idea of how he could be made happy.

She was thoughtful through the early and familiar stages of our dinner, but when

Margaret appeared with a cherry-speckled *mousse* she found inspiration.

"That special student in 'General Method'!" she announced. "She's the very thing for him."

"What do you know about her?" I asked with some surprise, for the woman had only just begun to attend lectures, and was a source of deep but ungratified curiosity to all of us. She always came in her motor car, and Marthana Caruth, who once helped her with her jacket, told us that it bore a Doucet label. She could read French and German authorities in the original — thus much we saw — and she was in mourning. She never took part in the discussions which often followed a lecture, never waited for a last confidential word with Professor Edwards, and never addressed more than the most formal of greetings to her nearest neighbours.

We guessed her to be the widow or the sister of a trustee. Bereaved ladies often sought to bury sorrow under learning in our midst, though never before had we enjoyed quite so perfect a specimen of the lady of leisure trying to interest herself in a subject which puzzled and bored her, but to which she gave the courteous attention proper to sermons and to "talks" by distinguished political strangers.

"She is gentle," Elizabeth pointed out; "presumably well off and unattached. Extremely well turned out and good looking, and not too intellectual to be admiring."

"And she's a good listener," I contributed. "But how are you going to bring them together?"

"I can't imagine," she answered. "That's the beauty of it."

Now if there is one possible fault in Elizabeth Alvord, considered in the light of friend and companion on the way to the Pierian spring, it is a tendency to assume at times the Sherlock Holmes attitude, and to force one to act Watson to her Sherlock. It is a most

She always came in her motor car

disagreeable trick, and when I see that she is playing it I always refuse to ask the ridiculous leading questions proper to my rôle, or to betray any amazement at the evidence and deductions she lays before me.

In this matter of Blaisdell's happy marriage, Elizabeth was soon forced to abandon her mysterious ways, and to take me into her confidence, because I, a promised Faculty bride, had a certain social standing which she lacked, and it was necessary that Miss Morton — we soon discovered that to be the special student's name — should be invited to tea. She came, and she was charming; she was good enough also to say that she was charmed, and to ask us to dine with her.

"Just we three," she explained. "Since my dear grandfather's death I entertain very little. You read perhaps of his death last September. He was motoring up from Long Island with a party of friends, and there was a collision."

We assured her that we had read of it. There had been automobile and train collisions in every Monday morning's paper from June to June, so we felt safe in saying that we remembered.

"I had taken care of him and of his house," she went on, "for fifteen years, and had been looking forward to doing so for years and years to come. He was not an old man!" she pointed out; "he was only eighty, and the doctor said that with the care I was giving him he might easily have lived to be a hundred."

"Of course he might," Elizabeth acquiesced heartily, "a grandfather of mine lived to be ninety-two without any particular care at all."

"And now," Miss Morton went on, "the days seem so long and so empty! There is nothing, absolutely nothing, for me to do, and I thought of studying a little about teaching, so that I might be useful in a mission which our church supports. But I don't," she explained, "seem to be getting on very rapidly, nor to understand very well."

"When I'm troubled," said Elizabeth, fixing a warning eye on me, "I find nothing so consoling and absorbing as painting or drawing," and she who in the days of her strength never went to a sketching class, unless dragged there in chains, launched forth into a panegyric upon the consolation to be found in colour and form. A panegyric more eloquent than any Blaisdell had ever delivered.

Elizabeth and I went with our guest to the elevator and, when her beautiful glossy black hat had sunk out of sight, we executed a triumphant war dance.

"She's the very thing!" cried Elizabeth, and I heartily agreed with her; "she has all the qualities which his wife must have, and added to them she has a passion for taking care of people."

"Bring them together now," said I.

Three days were to intervene between Miss Morton's having tea with us and our dining with her, and I devoted the afternoon of one of them to a reconnoitring tour. I was prepared for something solid and respectable in brownstone and high stoop, but I found instead a white marble affair with potted evergreens lavishly set forth upon its steps and glimpses of hot-house plants behind its lace-curtained windows. I hope Miss Morton was out at the time, for surprise transfixed me upon the opposite sidewalk. It was very evident that the late lamented grandfather had taken care of the granddaughter who had taken care of him. The Doucet gowns, the motor, the travels, and the friends to whom she had casually referred had all conveyed an impression of affluence, but the house said more than that.

Now it so chanced that we were asked to dine on Thursday, and Thursday is the night upon which Professor Blaisdell was wont to call upon Elizabeth. She had intended to ask him to come on Friday instead, but when I described the white marble house she decided to waste no time in further manœuvring but to bring her two characters together at once.

It seemed difficult enough in prospect, but in reality it worked out quite simply. John was going to some German lecture on his hobby, metaphysics, and he was easily cajoled into asking Blaisdell to act as his substitute, and to call for us at Miss Morton's house at about ten o'clock.

"Not that I have any idea," Elizabeth explained to me, "of leaving the scenes of revelry at such an early hour, but between seven o'clock and ten will give us lots of time to prepare Miss Morton's mind. And when Blaisdell arrives we can then and there arrange the drawing lessons."

The plan worked quite simply and beautifully. Miss Morton was prepared. The professor was introduced. The arrangement was made and Elizabeth was jubilant.

On the succeeding Monday morning a new drawing board, paint box, palette, and jar of brushes appeared upon the easel beside mine, and Miss Morton presently began some very creditable half-hour studies under the suave instruction of Professor Blaisdell, while Elizabeth, relieved from his persistent care, enjoyed French chocolates and Billy Blight's society.

Thereafter, when Blaisdell called, as he still conscientiously did, there was no talk of "perspective," "hieroglyphics," "atmosphere," or "brush work." The only art technicality remaining to him seemed to be "feeling," and the feelings most discussed were those of Elizabeth for Miss Morton. "She reminds me," that dutiful niece would remark with tears in her eyes and a quiver in her voice, "in so many ways of my dear Aunt Elizabeth. Have you noticed her eyes?"

Blaisdell had.

"Aunt Elizabeth's were just like that, large, dark, and full of feeling. Don't you think she has beautiful eyes?"

Blaisdell did.

"And then," Elizabeth would continue,

Miss Morton presently began some . . . studies under the suave instruction of Professor Blaisdell

"she looks at things in so much the way that Aunt Elizabeth did; the same high standards, you know, the same passion for the ideal."

Elizabeth used to repeat these conversations to me as soon as Blaisdell had left, but one night she went straight to her own room and I saw nothing of her until two or three hours later, when I awoke to find her sitting on the end of my bed in a flame-coloured Japanese kimono with her hair all hanging about her.

"Go away," said I, hospitably. "Can't you see that I am asleep?"

"I have that to tell," said she, "which will awake you. Professor Blaisdell has proposed for my lily-white hand."

"No!" I cried, aghast and awake, "it isn't possible."

"It's true," said she; "for all you know I may be now the affianced bride of a man" — and she dropped into sudden seriousness — "entirely too good for me. For he is good, Marion, good through and through."

"But not good for *you*," I parried.

"No," she admitted, "I know that, and I remembered it. I refused him."

"Did he take it well?"

"He took it," she was obliged to admit, "with a noble cheerfulness. He said that he would always think of me most kindly, and would always stand ready to fulfil the wishes of his dead friend, my aunt. That circumstances lately entering into his life had turned his mind toward marriage, and had made him see that others — perhaps I myself — had placed some serious interpretation upon the very great pleasure which he had evinced in my society. He said that if such were the case he should be honoured and happy to make my happiness the object of his life. Now is n't he the darling," she ended, "and can't you see what he means?"

"He has fallen in love with Miss Morton," I cried, "and he wanted to be sure that your welfare was in no way concerned.

My dear, I like him better than I ever thought it possible I should."

"So do I," said Elizabeth, as she kissed me. "He *will* be happier with Miss Morton, won't he?" she insisted a little wistfully. "You think so?"

"Oh, infinitely!" I answered.

At the door she halted. "Do you mind," she asked, "if I sleep in here with you to-night?"

Whatever doubts and regrets Elizabeth Alvord may have had that night — and we talked over a good many before she at last fell asleep — she had conquered them all next morning, and at noontime when we brought Miss Morton home to lunch with us — for Margaret was by this time quite herself again, and our *menus* were worthy even of Miss Morton's attention — Elizabeth was ready to make use of the event which had caused her so much perturbation.

"I wish very much," said she to our

guest when we had reached the time of conversation and salted almonds, "that you knew Professor Blaisdell better," and she threw a confidential glance at me; "we who know him well are very unhappy about him. Have you noticed how ill he is looking?"   `

Now he had n't been looking in the least ill, but the old care-taking spirit awakened in Miss Morton, and she said that she had noticed it for a week.

"He is ill," Elizabeth maintained, "absolutely ill. He is losing flesh rapidly, working entirely too hard, and yet not even to Professor Wentworth will he explain his trouble, or even admit that he *is* troubled. Now, if you were nearer, if you saw him oftener and more informally than you can in the studios or lecture room, you might be able to help us about him. You have had so much experience."

Of course Miss Morton swallowed it — bait, hook, sinker, float, line, and rod.

"Has he no one," she asked, "to take care of him?"

"No one at all," I answered. "He lives quite alone in his apartment: goes out to all his meals and is 'done for' by the janitor's wife. He was Professor Wentworth's friend years ago at Yale. He knows no one as well as he does us. I don't think," I added, wishing to show Elizabeth that I could coöperate when I would, "I don't think that he gets fresh air enough or change enough."

As we sat in silence waiting for this last suggestion to percolate to Miss Morton's kindly heart there sounded through our windows the honk of her motor's horn.

"I shall insist," said she, as she put on her gloves, "upon Professor Blaisdell coming out into the country with me this afternoon. There is nothing so important as health, and when my grandfather was quite young, only about seventy-five, he got himself to the point of nervous prostration by overwork. So you see I know all the symptoms, and just what to do, and I am old enough," she added, with a triumphant flush, for which I could have kissed her, "I'm old enough to take care of this young man and to do what I can to help him. My dears, I want to thank you for letting me help."

Again she vanished down the elevator shaft, and again Elizabeth and I were left jubilant.

"Isn't she a darling?" I broke out, and I suspected there were tears in my eyes.

"Aren't they a pair of darlings?" cried Elizabeth, and there was no doubt at all that there were tears in hers.

Now there are few things so sure as that a man will believe he is ill if he is told sufficiently often that he is looking so, and by the end of the week Miss Morton, Elizabeth, and I had produced something like panic in Professor Blaisdell. He cut down his hours of work so that he could go for motor trips in the afternoon; he went on a diet and he bought a Whitely exerciser. He believed implicitly that he was upon the verge of a nervous collapse, and the belief, naturally, made him very nervous.

The wedding occurred during the Easter recess. Elizabeth and I were bridesmaids, John was best man, and we, with the principals, comprised the bridal party of five. It was a very pretty, simple, and touching wedding, and did not at all seem to require the amount of explanation which has arisen round it. The first version is the bride's. She confided to me — you will notice in this story that nearly everyone confides in me; it's a way they have adopted since my engagement — that most of the courting had been on her side.

"I saw the chance for happiness," she explained, "and I took it, and I intend to make him as happy as he can make me."

Then came John with his account of

how all the Faculty had banded together
to drive Blaisdell into matrimony. He and
John were the only two marriageable bachelors
among the professors, and the others, knowing
John to be provided for, entered enthusiasti-
cally into a scheme to finish off Blaisdell.
They taught his classes, they listened to, nay,
they even insisted upon his confidences,
and at all times and seasons they extolled
the lady of his choice, and wished him joy.
Perhaps they were not all selfless in this
enthusiasm, for one or two of them, invited
to a casual dinner at Miss Morton's, felt
and inspired a very enthusiastic welcome for
this addition to the Faculty circle. Prexy,
in all seriousness, told John that they and
their colleagues were largely responsible for
the match.

Blaisdell's ideas contradicted both of these.
He expressed them at the Faculty dinner
given in his honour on the night before the
wedding, and John repeated them to us as he,
Elizabeth, and I drove to the church. "It

was the best speech," said John, "that any of us ever made, and that some of us ever heard. Everybody had been more or less joshing him, and he had been taking it like a lamb. He had only really made one speech before, and certainly the roars that greeted him when it was his turn might have upset a stump orator. 'Friends and fellow-travellers,' said he, 'I'm setting out upon the road by which you all have gone, but before this halo which has lassoed me becomes permanently affixed' —I wish you could have heard the fellows yell at that!" cried John. "Did you ever hear anything more neat?

"When at last we were quiet again he went on quite undisturbed. 'I have noticed, appreciated, and now I wish to thank you, for your efforts in my behalf during the last few months, but I want you to know' — here he stood very straight and looked very stern — 'I want you to know that I had a good deal more to do with what's going to happen to-morrow than you fellows seem to think.'

Then he sat down and then we went wild. Think of it! Blaisdell!"

"I'm thinking of it," said Elizabeth, and she did n't say much more before we reached the church.

The fourth responsibility was explained to me when Elizabeth and I, very tired, were having a cup of tea at the Grand Central Station, just after bidding adieu to the bridal pair. Elizabeth drew off her gloves and looked a little wistfully — or was it ruefully? — at me.

"You 'll never *say* anything to me," she pleaded, "if this day's work turns out ill, or if they do not 'live happy as you and I may'? I know that it was all my doing. I brought them together, I even selected them for one another, and whatever happens will be my fault, but you 'll never *say* so to me, will you, Marion?"

"I won't," I promised blithely, "because I won't think so. I think that the only responsible person in this affair was your Aunt Elizabeth."

IX

DIPLOMAS AND DIPLOMACY

M Y DEARS," cried Mrs. Pearson as she responded to our pressure of her hospitable electric bell, "my dears, this *is* a pleasant surprise."

It was a surprise to which she must have been growing accustomed, for Elizabeth and I — though fiercely independent as became our state — still craved the companionship of an older, wiser woman and the magic of a home. We found them all at the Pearson's and we spent all our disengaged Sundays and generally an evening or so a week in the haven of serenity which they had contrived by filling the drawing room and the dining room of their flat with low chairs deep and soft, a flood of pillows, a few divans, a *passé* piano; some prints, some lamps and the warmest, kindliest, most genuine hospitality to be found within a ten-mile radius of the campus. There was no surer help in times of trouble, no gladder congratulations in times of joy, no steadier friendship in steadier days than the Pearsons gave to such of us as were so fortunate as to be numbered among their friends. Trouble and responsibility seemed to touch them only through people they loved, yet I knew, and so did Elizabeth, that it was a hazardous and spirit-wearing task to maintain two small children and open house upon the salary attached to an assistant professorship.

"I think," she went on as she closed the door and led us into the tobacco-clouded living room, "that you ought to know everybody here. They 're all college people. I 'm not speaking of Billy Blight," she amended, as the tall figure of that young man with a twin Pearson clinging to each leg arose to salute us; "you *ought* not, of course, to know him, but I 'm afraid you do."

"Why, what 's he been a-doin' of?" asked

Elizabeth lightly, when we had greeted the other members of the party and taken our places among the faded pillows of a big divan.

"He's abused our hospitality!" Mrs. Pearson answered. "You know how we've given him the freedom of our new house, 'The Castle in Spain.' How we've let him wander about from room to room and look out of all the windows. You know how I even promised to let him paint frescoes on the nursery walls ——"

"Good safe place that," laughed Marthana Caruth, "the babies are too young to say what they think ——"

"But I must protest," said Professor Berger, a dear old chap from Jena who had come over to study American institutions and whom Prexy had shifted to Pearson's care for the afternoon — "it is important to the vitals that the young eye of the child shall not distorted be."

"Of course, of course," agreed all of us who retained the power of speech.

And Pearson did his young guest the justice and the honour to say, "Young Blight, Professor Berger, has won more medals and created more beauty than many an artist twice his age."

"But that does not excuse him," Mrs. Pearson interrupted. "His art may be good or bad, but his manners are atrocious. You know, dears," she went on, "how I've let him play billiards in the billiard room and read in the library."

We assured her that we did know; Billy had enjoyed, even as Elizabeth and I had done, the free range of the blue prints for the Pearsons' proposed house at West Farms. The plans were even now lying in an untidy roll under the mission table. Mrs. Pearson picked them up and spread them for our inspection.

"See what he's done," she cried dramatically, while Billy muttered something about self-defence.

"Oh, that *is* too bad of him," cried Elizabeth. "Marthana, Mr. Rollins, do come and see what Billy Blight's done to the very best bedroom in the house."

We gathered round her and there we read across the fair space of the room over the library, "Reserved for the exclusive use of William Blight, Esquire."

"Oh, really, Billy, that is too bad of you," I cried; "that's the room I fixed on for myself."

"And I," said Elizabeth.

"And I," echoed Marthana.

"And we," said Mrs. Pearson.

"That's right, butting in, all of you," growled Billy. "No privacy even in a chap's own room. I'll not visit you at all. No, not if you were to let me sleep in the butler's pantry, with all the cupboards full of goodies and the ice-box within easy reach. 'It's a long worm that has no turning.' The inhospitality and the selfishness with which I have been treated this day are the last two straws ——"

"'T was a camel, not a worm, that suffered

from last straws," Elizabeth corrected him heartlessly, and then bedlam reigned.

Presently John came in. Although he is younger than Pearson the two are great friends and I think that it is partly on this account that Mrs. Pearson is so good to me. She knows that I shall some day be a Faculty wife, and she already treats me with the confidence and friendship which characterizes most of the men and women who supply the mental grist to our mill. They are nearly all young; they are all ambitious; and they are more independent than such a body generally is because Prexy is so much away from the college. He is our publicity man — every institution in these days must have one — and he is always off lecturing, attending conferences, serving on commissions, getting us new trustees or endowments. This leaves the ordinary day by day administration of affairs in the hands of the other men and brings them into frequent and intimate association with one another.

So when John had smoked a quiet pipe and

entertained our Germanic friend for half an hour, it seemed quite natural that Mr. Pearson and he should retreat to a tiny room, called by courtesy the study, in which our host kept a few books and bones. Pearson's speciality was zoölogy. Presently Mrs. Pearson and I were summoned to join them and Professor Berger was left to be amused and mystified by the youngsters.

"Dear friends," said Mrs. Pearson, when the door was closed. "We have *such* news. I 've been dying to tell you out there. You know how long we 've had those plans and yet how far we seemed from laying the corner-stone, so to speak."

"Of course they do, dear," Pearson interrupted — "don't they know we 've always spoken of it as the 'Castle in Spain' ?"

"Bless it!" cried the future châtelaine.

"Well," continued Pearson, and his earnest face and a little break in his voice made the words beautiful to us who were so fond of him, "I see my way clear at last and I 've signed the contract. I'm to pay for the Castle in two years. If we're careful ——"

"And oh! we shall be careful!" breathed his wife.

"We may own it all in eighteen months."

Of course we congratulated them jubilantly and Pearson went on:

"It's all on account of that course of zoölogy which the President is listed to conduct. I'm to have that next year. He spoke of it last week. That will raise me to a full professorship. My salary will increase by two thousand dollars, I shall be the head of the Science Department and just about the proudest and happiest fellow between here and Timbuctoo."

Again we tumultuously congratulated him.

"And it isn't only that," he went on, "not only the money, though God knows that will be welcome enough; not the house, though that will be precious enough; not the position, though that will be fine enough. But it's the work! The chance! A great big chance to do great big work. I 'll make the department a wonder. I 'll make the chaps in other universities — aye, and in other countries like that Berger there — I 'll make 'em sit up and take notice. And ah, the students I 'll turn out!"

"No, Robert," cried his wife taking his hand in hers — "you 'll never turn out any students at all. You 'll get so attached to them and so interested in them and they 'll get so devoted to you that you 'll all stay there together, one great happy family, dabbling in the internal workings of the animal kingdom. What makes you look so serious, fair Marion?" she asked, suddenly turning to me. "What 's the matter, child?"

"I 'm thinking how I should love to be there," I answered; "but I was born too soon. I 'm a senior you know, and all these plans are for next year when I shan't be there. And we 're having *such* an awful time! Prexy away and the most awful substitute doing the work — you 've heard of it, I know."

Of course they had. They all knew what

we suffered under Doctor Archibald. Like
the man in the poem: "His beard was weedy,
his hair was long, and weedy and long was he."
Also he delivered his lectures, "in a singular
minor key." He just burbled along from
subject to subject and we trailed after him if
we chanced to be awake. He was unquestion-
ably learned, but he was no less unquestion-
ably incapable of imparting his learning. His
lectures came late in the afternoon of Monday,
Thursday and Friday, a bad time for even a
proficient instructor, but fatal to a bad one.
Everyone was always tired and weariness,
acting on our different natures in different
ways, reduced the Senior Class to a mixture
of irritability, frivolity, physical exhaustion,
indifference, and animosity. Dr. Archibald's
platitudinous statements fell upon this remarkably bad ground and bore fruit sometimes in
an inattentive lassitude; contagious, overwhelming, and impenetrable, and sometimes
in acrimonious criticism or retort, leading to
general and disgraceful uproar.

Now, neither Elizabeth nor I cared very much whether we made our début in the world learned or unlearned in the matter of zoölogy. As students in the art department the course was prescribed for us as a sort of ground work in general structure and anatomy. We never expected to teach the thing and to us our marks in it, whether for themes or even for the final examination looming toward us at the end of the year, mattered comparatively little. But the case of the majority of the students was very different. They expected, most of them, to fill positions as superintendents, principals, teachers and even professors and possibly their diplomas — but surely their ability to pass a creditable general examination — would be influenced by their knowledge or ignorance of the natural sciences. All these things they sat and thought of while Archibald read us his musty old lectures, and laid waste four and a half precious hours a week.

Things were at this pass when a peripatetic

lecturer named Thorneycroft bloomed out one day on the bulletin board with announcements of an extension lecture on "Embryonic Traits." It was one of those popular illuminated and illuminating things which the Board of Trustees arranged for us from time to time. Prexy returned from a two months' absence just in time to preside and the thing was a great success. The lecture was everything which poor old Archibald's ought to be and were not. The contrast was dazzling, and even Billy Blight could not believe that he 'd been listening to a dissertation on poor despised zoölogy.

The lecture was one of a course of three, to be delivered at varying intervals, and it dawned upon one of the interfering "Eds" to write Prexy a petition to engage Thorneycroft to take our zoölogy class for the rest of the year. There was no definite criticism of Archibald, but the implication was there. We were all delighted at the prospect — we all signed the petition and awaited results. Prexy had always been strong on public sentiment and "the pulse of the student body" — used to harangue the other men about the authority of *Vox Populi*. He, who never stayed with us long enough to hear it! But when he got it written out, signed and sealed, he set about obeying it.

It was two or three weeks after this that the little routine of our daily lives was upset by John's arrival in the afternoon, while Elizabeth and I were wrestling with the Life and Times of Leonardi da Vinci. John hardly ever came to see me in the afternoon and his face, as Margaret ushered him into the little drawing room, was so grave that Elizabeth prepared to beat a retreat.

"I want to talk to you both," he began, when we had established him in the Morris chair. "I have sent for Billy Blight; he'll be here presently. There's something very serious in the air."

"Has Billy broken out again?" I questioned, but John shook his head.

"More serious, far," he answered and just at that moment Billy's cheerful boots resounded in our hall.

"What's up?" he questioned with instant concern when he saw the gravity in our little group.

"I'm afraid Pearson's chance is up," John answered. "I've seen it coming on for two or three weeks—ever since the president came back. But now I'm afraid it's certain."

"His chance?" repeated Elizabeth. "You don't mean the 'Castle in Spain'?"

"I mean his promotion — his increase — everything. I'm going to tell you three — two of you the wildest youngsters in the college — and the third the wisest and dearest — a grave Faculty secret. My reason is that we four are perhaps the best friends the Pearsons have and they'll be needing friendship, I'm afraid. You know about that petition to the president; well, he acted upon it and Thorneycroft has consented on condition that he be given full professorship next year and be made head of the Science Department. Now Pearson has never had a definite agreement with the president or the trustees. There seemed to be no need of any. And he, poor old chap, was acting entirely on his own responsibility when he made so sure of it. There is no reason under the sun why Thorney-croft's proposition should not be accepted. He is better known than Pearson. His name and his titles will read well in the catalogue."

"But have n't you," I asked, "all of you who appreciate Mr. Pearson, have n't you remonstrated with Prexy?"

"He ought to have his face pushed?" Billy was understood to contribute.

"Surely, surely," answered John. "We 've said all that 's possible, but the president, when he is riding his *Vox Populi, Vox Dei* hobby, is not amenable to arguments. It looks very much as if the thing would go through."

"And the castle in Spain," wailed Elizabeth, "the darling castle in Spain."

"Will stay in Spain I fear," said John, as he rose and resumed his overcoat. "I must get back to a lecture. It's not the first time that *Vox Populi* has incited murder."

For some space after John left us Elizabeth, Billy, and I sat and gulped in despair. It seemed impossible that plans so kind and helpful as those of the Pearsons could be all broken and trampled down by Archibald's inefficiency. We were marvelling thus and sitting dejectedly over the tea and cake which Margaret's hospitality had provided when there entered unto us the one person in the world whom we were least prepared to face.

"Mrs. Pearson, Miss Marion," Margaret announced, and before we could gather our scattered wits, she was looking at us out of her dear, old, friendly, unsuspecting eyes, and settling herself down, cozily assured of welcome.

"It *is* luck finding you here," she assured Billy — "I was going to write you a line to-night. For you three dear children — and

John, of course, Marion — must come to
Spain on Saturday week for the laying of the
cornerstone. The castle is actually going up."

"My God," murmured Billy.

"Stop your profanity, sir," she chided him.
"I can't imagine what your parents or guar-
dians were thinking of to let you acquire it."

My throat was actually stiff, but in the dusk
I managed to squeeze it and to force myself
into some kind of articulation.

"Of course we'll all be in Spain when the
cornerstone is laid," I mumbled.

"You've got a cold, dear," she broke in
promptly, "I'll have a word or two with
Margaret about you as I go out. You know,
I hate to think of any of the students being
sick here in town. That's going to be one of
my great joys in the castle. I shall always
have a convalescent or two sitting out over
the portcullis and getting well in the sunshine."
She halted for a moment, but as none of us
felt equal to a remark she went on again in
her own whimsical, delightful way.

"The moat will be full of formaldehyde. A yellow flag shall float over the battlements; the drawbridge will be always up and the iron-studded oaken doors covered thick with scarlet fever plasters."

Elizabeth achieved something which in the darkness passed for a laugh.

"And now I'm going. I just dropped in to make sure of you for the cornerstone. The babies will be wondering where I am if I stay any longer. And if Robert reached home and found no one to greet him but Maria, I verily believe he'd go away again and think he did n't live there at all."

Presently she was gone and we three were left together, at the mercy of our nerves and our imaginations until Billy Blight broke out with:

"I can stand anything but the powers of darkness. Let's have a light on this thing," and when he had his light he found that both Elizabeth and I were crying.

I think Margaret fed us. I think Billy

stayed to dinner. I think we all talked spasmodically in queer trailing little spurts, but I don't remember anything very distinctly until Billy rose to go away.

"And hang it all," he cried, suddenly, as the personal application occurred to him for the first time, "that bounder of a Thorneycroft will work us all to death. How are we going to do in twelve weeks the work that ought to have been spread over nine months. And if we don't make up the stuff, he'll throw us all down on the exam. And we'll all be back here next year looking at the dear old Pearsons and knowing that we — for did n't we sign that petition — have shut them out of Spain. Oh Lord! oh Lord!"

I had read of sleepless nights, but I don't think I ever experienced one till then. Hour after hour I revolved the dilemma and studied all its horrid horns. There seemed nothing to do; absolutely nothing to do. And yet I was on fire to help my friends, and to show John that I could be trusted not only as a safe confidant but as a resourceful ally. It was six o'clock and the gray morning was looking in through the windows when at last I hit upon a plan and pattered in to awake Elizabeth and discuss it with her. She, too, had slept but badly, and had no more practical measure to suggest than to bribe an anarchist to blow up Prexy. When I pointed out to her that in relieving us of Prexy, the bomb might also deprive us of the College, she was quite disheartened. But then she was never half herself until she had her morning coffee.

"Now what I thought is this," I began as I pulled her eiderdown about my shoulders, "we'll just frighten these 'Eds' away from Thorneycroft and back to poor old Archibald."

"But how?" she questioned.

"I got the idea from Billy. You remember what he said, just before he went, about all the extra work and time which the change would involve and the likelihood of our losing our diplomas in the end. Billy generally talks nonsense, but he was as sensible as a judge then. If we can once get the men students — and the majority of women students, too, for that matter—to see this aspect of the case, I think you 'll see them flocking back to Prexy, and declaring themselves quite satisfied with poor old Archibald, who, even if he does not teach us very much, certainly makes no unreasonable demands upon our time and, just as certainly, will give us all an easy exam and good marks at the end."

"You 're a darling and a genius," cried Elizabeth. "It shall certainly be done. We 'll make 'em cry for Archibald before the week 's over. But now let 's sleep a little; it is n't quite time to get up."

When public opinion sets strongly in one direction it is no easy thing for three youngsters — however strong their enthusiasm and however disinterested their aim — to turn it round again. And we had to be very, very careful. It would never have done to show hostility. We were just plaintively natural; aware of our mental inferiority; crushed by it; but resigned to it.

"Oh, yes of course," Elizabeth would sweetly agree when some enthusiastic "Ed" was singing Thorneycroft's praises. "Of course, it's all very well for you. You're clever, but I know I shall not get my diploma this year. I've heard something of Professor Thorneycroft's plans" — Oh subtle, sly Elizabeth — "He's going to rush us through the whole subject in the next eleven weeks. Then we're to have one week for review and a comprehensive examination to finish off with. It *will* finish me. Dead. There'll be no diploma for me this year. Ah well, another year seems long, but it will pass."

That was all very well for Elizabeth Alvord, young, independent, and with no responsibilities in the world. Her being at college at all was a whim of hers. Her leaving without a diploma and degree or her staying to work another year for them were matters of pleasure or convenience with her. No more.

But to the men with their way to make in
the not too affluent world of teaching the
prospect of another year without appointment
and salary was a serious thing.

"And I don't think," Elizabeth would go
on, taking off her cap and rumpling her pretty
hair, in a distracted fashion, "that poor old
Dr. Archibald is bad enough to make all this
necessary. If would be a terrible thing for
him to be dismissed like this in the middle of
the semester. And has n't it seemed to you,"
she would add, with the prettiest air of deference, "that his lectures are getting a little
better? Of course, I'm no judge. I'm
very ignorant. But don't you think that he
is getting in a little more subject-matter?"

And the "Ed" would be forced to agree.
Billy in a desperate last attempt to steer us all
to Spain had invited Archibald and Pearson to
dine with him and had gently started Pearson
on his pet theories. It was impossible for
anyone to listen unmoved and unenlightened
to his clear enthusiasms; and Archibald

absorbed clarity and power enough to transfigure his two or three succeeding lectures.

We worked quietly, but we worked hard. And gradually — very gradually — the leaders in the movement to oust Archibald found themselves with few followers and less sympathy. Faculty meetings generally took place on Thursday, and on the Thursday preceding the Saturday fixed for the laying of the cornerstone, John again surprised me by calling upon me in the afternoon.

"I have n't a moment to stay," he explained. "I 've just come to tell you of a most extraordinary thing. Nearly all the men and several of the women who signed poor Pearson's death-warrant have gone to the president and asked him to reconsider any idea of change in the Science Department."

"*Vox Populi* changing its tune," said I, and was preparing to confess to the conspiracy and my part in it when Elizabeth and Billy Blight, crowned with almost visible laurels, broke in upon us. Billy grasped John's hand and shook it warmly, while Elizabeth gathered me into her embrace.

"Is n't it wonderful?" they cried in chorus.

"And is n't Marion wonderful?" Elizabeth added.

"What are you two lunatics talking about?" John demanded, and Elizabeth was so breathlessly victorious that she perforce allowed Billy to do the talking.

"Thorneycroft's down and out. Prexy 'learns that the feeling of the undergraduate body has changed.' Told us so in a nice little speech in his office when I went in with two or three other chaps to speak my little piece. It would have drawn tears to the eye of a graven image to hear me telling him how we had all learned to love and reverence Archibald. How it was only his preliminary lecture that went a little above our heads."

"Marvellous," murmured John, "marvellous and unaccountable."

"And we can go to West Farms on Saturday," cried Elizabeth, "with easy minds and

consciences.   The Pearsons are safe.   If the
castle were finished now we four might crave
its hospitality on account of the brain strain it
has caused us.   Oh, you dear old Marion!"
she cried, and again threw her arms around
me — while Billy again shook John effusively
by his unresisting hand.

"She's a girl in a thousand," Mr. Blight
was pleased to assure my fiancé.   "She'll
make a wife in a million."

"I know it well," John acquiesced, "but
might I trouble you to explain why you hold
her responsible for this change in public
opinion?"

"Oh, it's only their nonsense, John dear,"
I answered.   "We've done nothing; nothing
at all; except to give a few singing lessons to
Vox Populi."

X

THE FINALS

THE attitude of the whole college toward Elizabeth was most extraordinary. The Faculty, even with the business-encrusted Prexy, seemed to emulate the semi-apologetic, semi-exasperated sentiments of the hen who finds one duck among a dozen more normal offspring. As for the rest of us: well, we were just barnyard chickens scratching for "culture" from dawn to dark while she floated off on some flower-bordered river and could not be recalled by any amount of clucking on the part of the authorities.

There was no one for her to play with, no one else, I verily believe, except the kindergarten experts in the art, who knew how to play. Yet instead of disapproving of her reprehensible idleness we fell to devising schemes for her amusement and excuses for her many wanderings from the way, hard and narrow, which leads to diplomas.

Billy Blight was another student on whom the shackles of college laws sat lightly. He, however, chose other scenes in which to give his individuality free scope and, as I have said, it was some time before he and Elizabeth appreciated one another. When at last an understanding was seen to grow between them we were overjoyed. Surely, we told ourselves and one another, she would now forsake the primrose path of dalliance and, leaving college rules and bylaws at peace, devote her talents to the subjugation of Billy. So we thought in our new and book-shop psychology. And we were right on one point — the subjugation. It occurred as per schedule, but it was accompanied with such crashes through academic usage as had never, in the memory of the oldest janitor, dotted our annals.

As breach after breach of discipline shook our halls it came about that Miss Alvord and Mr. Blight were rather constantly together. There was nothing suspicious, nothing alarming, in this companionship and there was certainly — as John and I admitted to one another — nothing in the least sentimental.

Billy fell into the habit of spending a good many evenings in the apartment. Such was, also, John's pleasant custom. And as the weeks went on creating no break in our quartette, John and I began to think that there was no ground for our fears that Elizabeth would some time go too far for the Faculty's latitude, and that Billy would go with her. What we elders — and those two youngsters made us perforce mature — what we two elders dreaded for them was expulsion before the final examinations or failure in them. John as a member of the Faculty considered the college diploma with a respectful eye, something to be worked for and held as an honour in the world of men. And I, his

fond and affianced bride, was not likely to
differ from him. In vain, and yet not perhaps quite in vain, we lectured the delin-
quents as tactfully as our great liking for them
prompted. Their conduct cannot have been
said to benefit in any marked degree, but
they certainly devoted themselves to text
books, notebooks, summaries, and lectures
with a new respect. Elizabeth, I say with
no pride of sex or friendship, was the cleverer
of the two, and between them they made out
a sort of synopsis of each of the difficult
subjects in our course. They had two copies
of each struck off and they studied them
unceasingly. It was undeniably a sort of
slow and lazy "cramming," and it is wonderful how proficient they became. It was only
necessary to mention a heading to one of
them and lo, the fount of their learning
flowed clear; full of facts and dates, names
and technicalities, full of cause and effect;
history and philosophy. As Billy beamingly
remarked to John when he had read aloud

their ground plan on English literature, "can anybody beat us when we sally into the examination room with that, word for word, in our little hearts?"

And the word-for-word boast was no idle one. They could go on and on and on in a sort of parrot monotone, and they knew, too, exactly what it all meant, for they used to sit and wrangle about it in our little drawing room until Margaret, who saw a potential courtship in every caller, was quite scandalized.

Nearer and nearer loomed the finals. Paler and paler grew post-graduate and under-graduate brow. Shakier and shakier grew educational and co-educational nerve. All the lectures were reviews. All the students were wrecks; all save Elizabeth Alvord and Billy Blight, who were actually seen to eat roast beef and baked potatoes one hour before the time set for an examination. They possessed, they were kind enough to assure the suffering, the only digestion and the only working system on the campus.

For three days this went on; and on the morning of the fourth it percolated through chapel, lecture hall, and corridor, that Miss Alvord and Mr. Blight had been expelled in full and special meeting of the Faculty on a charge of cribbing, proved and confessed.

Cribbing! the meanest, vilest, most underhand of all the crimes against college law. An offence which no sympathy could reach, no friendship condone. That Billy and Elizabeth should be even charged with it was infamous, unbelievable. They in their evertriumphant career had inevitably given cause for much heart-burning, jealousy and envy, and yet there was not one in all the college who believed them capable or guilty of cribbing.

Proved! The professor in charge at the examination in history of education had seen that Miss Alvord had finished and handed in her paper with great celerity. Shortly afterward in walking about the room he saw a piece of paper slide under the door of the cloak room. Mr. Blight was seated near the door. He must have been watching for the paper. Upon its appearance he stooped instantly and stuck it into his coat pocket. Feeling that one of the culprits was secure the professor went instantly into the hall and locked the outer door of the cloak room, the only way by which the second offender might escape except by passing through the class room. Mr. Blight had written steadily for almost an hour and had then laid his paper upon the professor's desk. The professor, the justest and kindliest of men, told Billy what he had observed and demanded an explanation, the crib, and the name of his accomplice. Billy refused all.

"Then I will show the accomplice to you," said Johnson. "I am afraid, Mr. Blight, that there is no course open to me except to report this matter to the Faculty. And I want you to believe that I know you could explain it if you would and that you are now doing yourself, and will probably force my colleagues to do you, a great injury. We shall now see who is behind the door from which that paper came." When he discovered his brightest and favourite student, defiant among the hats and coats and rubbers, he nearly wept.

But when late in the evening he was forced to make his formal charge before a special Faculty meeting, with Billy and Elizabeth in attendance, he had himself well in hand and presented his evidence clearly. Billy's receipt of the paper. Elizabeth's presence in the cloak room. The identity in thought and arrangement of their examination papers. Before he sat down he turned to Prexy with a queer whimsical twist in his mouth:

"I saw these things. As was my duty I reported them. Yet I firmly believe that there is some entirely honourable explanation and that these young people have some good and kindly reason for withholding it."

I, who had been admitted at Elizabeth's request, was seated near the door and from my place the whole scene was like something in a play. The brilliant lights, the eager faces starting out of the surrounding gloom, the dignity and the earnestness of word and attitude made it almost impossible for me to realize John and quite impossible to believe that the two figures, seated at the end of the table, were indeed our careless, care-free Billy and Elizabeth. She was grave and a little whiter than her habit was. He half defiant, half impatient, yet forcibly self-restrained. They kept their eyes fixed on Johnson during his address and at his little valedictory they flushed with frankest gratitude. When he resumed his place they turned again to Prexy.

"You have heard," said he, "the charge against you and the evidence upon which it is founded. I agree with Professor Johnson's opinion that the charge is false and that neither of you has borrowed knowledge from the other. All present agreeing with this view, will say 'Aye.'"

"Aye," said everyone. I was so excited that I said it myself.

"Nevertheless," Prexy went on, "I, like Professor Johnson, have a duty to perform. Two students of our institution have been detected in the act of cribbing. The evidence is conclusive and it only remains to ask Miss Alvord whether it be exact, whether she handed a paper to Mr. Blight and whether that paper contained matter pertinent to the examination then proceeding."

"I did," announced Elizabeth, "slip such a paper under the door."

"And you, Mr. Blight," said Prexy, "did you receive such a paper?"

"I did," said Billy.

"Is there any explanation, Miss Alvord, that you care to make of this extraordinary occurrence?"

"None," she answered.

"And you? Mr. Blight, do you wish to explain?"

"I cannot, sir," said Billy.

There was a protracted silence after this, and then three or four of the professors who knew the culprits best gathered around Prexy. John was among them, and Blaisdell. Even old Johnson and Poppy Ames.

"Get them to explain," was Prexy's ultimatum. They tried it, but Billy and Elizabeth, serious-eyed and apparently five years older since the morning, could only shake their heads and drive their adherents to puzzlement and wrath.

Then Prexy struck the table with his gavel and stood up.

"It only remains for me to declare Miss Elizabeth Alvord and Mr. William Blight expelled from the college until such time as they offer sufficient refutation of the charge against them."

There was still some trace of Billy's manner, so bright and debonair, as he turned to Elizabeth, and, although her face expressed dismay, alarm, and intense chagrin, there was no falter of guilt in her pretty eyes as she rose and stood beside him. The men moved in in a group toward the door and me and, as the culprits passed between, many were the kindly handshakes they received, many the expressions of incredulity. Finally, only our quartette was left, and as we walked toward the apartment — I might as well admit that I was whimpering — John held me back a moment, and whispered:

"All they wanted, dear, was a little trouble. They're going through it now, and it will bring them closer together than all their daredeviltry ever could."

"You seem to be right," said I, as we came upon a little group under the campus trees. It was Mr. Blight, distraught and wild-eyed, yet all tender of his burden and Miss Elizabeth Alvord weeping in his arms with her head buried against his shoulder and one convulsive hand clutching him by the necktie.

"I believe," said Billy, as we approached, "'pon my honour, I believe she's crying."

"Of course she is," John acquiesced, "and," disregarding all the youth's signals of distress, "as you don't want us, we'll just run down to

Murray's and have a little supper. Tell Margaret not to keep anything for us. You and Elizabeth must be starved. Run along now. We'll talk over this other matter to-morrow."

An inarticulate sound from the neighbourhood of Billy's breast pocket reproached this heartlessness. I felt that we deserved much greater berating and might have stayed to essay comfort had not John hurried me away with a determined hand.

"Leave them to one another and to trouble," advised this practical philosopher.

"And to Margaret," I added, taking heart of grace.

"She'll be good for them," said he; "she'll bear it worse than they do. And my dear Marion," he went on as we set out for the hospitable lights of Murray's, "I think that we need have no further anxiety about Elizabeth. She's not the kind of girl to weep on a promiscuous shoulder."

Followed two or three days of horrible

helplessness and of hourly wrestles with Elizabeth. She would weep, she would laugh. She would pet me or make much of Margaret, · but she would not say one word or syllable which might be construed into an explanation. She even pretended to chortle over me as I went forth to examination after examination, contrasting my condition of servitude with her freedom. I grew quite accustomed to returning at luncheon time or in the afternoon to be met with Margaret's, "Gone out with Mr. Blight." This was occasionally varied with an extremely confidential, "Mr. Blight and Miss Elizabeth are in the drawing room."

I don't wish to convey the impression that they were utterly callous and shameless. They were not. They grieved constantly and very sincerely, but I think they were much more concerned by our concern than by any that tortured their own secretive breasts.

Four days passed. Examinations had still a week to run and Commencement was still two weeks away, and the president summoned us all to a special meeting in the Chapel. He looked positively jubilant.

"Ladies and gentlemen," he began, after the usual preliminaries. "It is not often that justice, being, as we all know, blind, moves quickly. But it is my privilege this morning to undo an act of injustice which has endured for only four days. A letter from a member of the undergraduate body, no longer with us, reached me last night, giving the explanation which a quixotic sense of honour and loyalty inspired Miss Alvord and Mr. Blight to withhold from us. The circumstances are these. Beside Miss Alvord in the examination room sat a student with whom she had long been on interested and friendly terms. Seeing that this friend laboured under difficulties, Miss Alvord, finishing her own paper went to her locker, got out her synopsis of the subject and slipped it under the door close to Mr. Blight, with a scribbled line upon it directing him to hand it to this other student. The rest of the story you all know. The friend passed this examination but failed in so many others that no hope remained as to the final outcome. All this is explained in the letter which was laid before the Faculty last night. The unaccountable occurrences of last Monday are now understood, and it only remains for me publicly to exonerate Mr. Blight from all suspicion — though suspicion never really existed. In Miss Alvord's case, it is the decision of the Faculty that although she broke a very stringent rule of college ethics, she did so unselfishly and has probably been already sufficiently punished. We therefore consider the incident closed. Miss Alvord and Mr. Blight are again students in good standing."

I rushed home and told Billy and Elizabeth who were studying continental maps in the dining room.

"Now is n't that glorious news?" I cried. "Ah! you mad, bad children!"

"We have news, too," said Elizabeth, and added with her first and last blush:

"You tell her, Billy."

XI

CASTLES IN SPAIN

WE have three teeth," announced Mrs. William Blight proudly.

"Teeth are nothing," I replied; "Richard the Third was born with a full set of them. But *we* can walk."

"Not really!" cried Elizabeth.

"Really!" I answered, and softened by her humbler attitude I went on, "Young Morton Blaisdell has no teeth at all, and can't walk a step, yet they are perfectly delighted with him and consider him a true type of the eleven months' old Che-ild."

"By the way," asked Elizabeth, turning to Mrs. Pearson, "are the Blaisdells to be here to-day?"

"I think I hear them arriving now," she answered, and hurried off in a hospitable flutter.

Again it was Sunday afternoon, and again we were assembled at the Pearsons. It seemed impossible, looking at Elizabeth, to realize that much time and many events separated this Sunday afternoon from that other one when the Castle in Spain had been only a ragged sheaf of blue prints. For now its stately walls smiled at the newcomer with their peaceful shingles already appreciably weather-stained. While the moat — if the sunken garden could be so considered — held nothing more formidable than a wealth of flowers and the Pearson twins.

With the arrival of the Blaisdells we took on the air almost of a Faculty meeting. For here were gathered together Professor Pearson, head of the Science Department; Professor Blaisdell, head of the Art Department, and Professor Wentworth, head of the Department of Philosophy and Education.

"It 's awfully good of you three chaps," said Billy humbly, "to let a duffer like me come out here and listen to you elevating of your minds on mental airships."

"Nonsense, Billy," cried his loyal consort. "It's awfully good of us to come back and listen to them again after all we suffered at college. Come over here, Mrs. Blaisdell," she went on, "and be comfy and ignorant with me. What *do* you think! Wilhelmina has three teeth!"

"Three!" echoed Mrs. Blaisdell, satisfactorily impressed.

"In very sooth in truth," broke in the proud father. "Came up like daisies in the night. Never was more surprised in my life than when she laughed and showed me the first."

"They are such an obsession with him," Elizabeth informed us, "that I expect him to do a whole frieze of them in his next commission. Did he tell you, Mr. Blaisdell," and she turned to the professor, "that they have given him the new courthouse on the upper west side?"

"And you call yourself a duffer!" laughed Blaisdell, shaking his old pupil by the hand. John and Mr. Pearson and all the rest of us followed his example with great cordiality.

"Then I suppose," said Mrs. Pearson, "that we shall some day be peeling the wall off the nursery and selling it at so much per inch as an example of the early manner of the famous William Blight."

"I can't call him a great success at nurseries," Elizabeth admitted. "He did one for Wilhelmina, and the result is such that it's the loveliest room in the house, used as the family living room, while its rightful occupant 'moves on' from bedroom to bedroom."

"Well, let us hope," said Pearson, "that he will catch the spirit of the tribunal more happily."

"Courts and things like that," the young artist protested, "always give me the shivers since the night that Elizabeth and I faced all you chaps about that cribbing thing. I never felt so horrid in my life. That was on account of Elizabeth's being there. But you never know how things will turn out. If we had n't been there together we might n't be here together. By Jove!" he added, taking the empty chair beside his wife and laying his hand on hers, "I never thought of that. No Elizabeth! No Wilhelmina! Nothing at all, by George!"

THE END

Lightning Source UK Ltd.
Milton Keynes UK
UKHW011444100119
335176UK00012B/1401/P